SCIENCE FICTION

This is a volume in the
Arno Press collection

SCIENCE FICTION

ADVISORY EDITORS

R. Reginald

Douglas Menville

See last pages of this volume
for a complete list of titles

THE MAN WHO
MASTERED TIME

RAY CUMMINGS

ARNO PRESS

A New York Times Company

New York — 1975

Reprint Edition 1974 by Arno Press Inc.

SCIENCE FICTION
ISBN for complete set: 0-405-06270-2
See last pages of this volume for titles.

Manufactured in the United States of America

—————•—————

Library of Congress Cataloging in Publication Data

Cummings, Ray.
    The man who mastered time.

    (Science fiction)
    Reprint of the 1930 ed. published by A. L. Burt,
Chicago.
    I. Title. II. Series.
PZ3.C9125Man12 [PS3505.U339] 813'.5'2 74-15960
ISBN 0-405-06270-2

THE MAN WHO
MASTERED TIME

THE MAN WHO MASTERED TIME

By RAY CUMMINGS

A. L. BURT COMPANY

Publishers   New York

Published by arrangement with A. C. McClurg & Co.

Printed in U. S. A.

Printed In The United States of America

To those many magazine readers
who have so kindly applauded
my work this book is gratefully
dedicated.

Ray Cummings.

CONTENTS

THE MAN WHO
MASTERED TIME

CHAPTER I.
A STRANGE PROJECT.

"TIME," said George, "why I can give you a definition of time. It's what keeps everything from happening at once."

A ripple of laughter went about the little group of men.

"Quite so," agreed the Chemist. "And, gentlemen, that's not nearly so funny as it sounds. As a matter of fact, it is really not a bad scientific definition. Time and space are all that separate one event from another. Everything happens some*where* at some*time*."

"You intimated you had something vitally important to tell us," the Big Business Man suggested. "Something, Rogers, that would amaze us. Some project you were about to undertake —"

Rogers raised his hand. "In a moment, gentlemen. I want to prepare you first — to some extent, at least. That's why I have led you into this discussion. I want you to realize that your preconceived

1

ideas of time are wrong—inadequate. You must think along entirely different lines, in terms of, I shall say, the *new science*."

"*I* will," agreed George. "Only tell me how."

"You said that time, space, and matter are not separate, distinct entities, but are blended together," the Doctor declared. "Just what do you mean?"

Rogers gazed earnestly about the room. "This, my friends. Those are the three factors which make up our universe as we know it. I said they were blended. I mean that the actual reality underlying all the manifestations we experience is not temporal or spatial or material, but a blend of all three. It is we who, in our minds, have split up the original unity into three such supposedly different things as time, space and matter."

"Take space and time," said the Big Business Man. "Those two seem wholly different to me. I shouldn't think they had the slightest connection."

"But they have. Between the three planes of space —length, breadth and thickness—and time, there is no essential distinction. We think of them differently—we instinctively feel differently about them.

2

But science is not concerned with our feelings — and science recognizes to-day that time is a property of space, just as are length, breadth and thickness."

"That's easy to say," growled the Banker. "Any one can make statements that can't be proved."

"It has been proved," Rogers declared quietly. "The mathematical language of science would bore you. Let me give you a popular illustration — an illustration, by the way, that I saw in print long before Einstein's theory was made public. For instance, think about this: A house has length, breadth and thickness. The house is matter, and it has three dimensions of space. But what else has it?"

A blank silence followed his sudden question.

"Hasn't it duration, gentlemen? Could a house have any real existence if it did not exist for any time at all?"

"Gosh," said George. "That's so. *I* never thought of that."

Rogers went on calmly: "You must admit, my friends, that matter depends for its existence on time equally as on space. They are, as I said, blended together. A house must have length, breadth, thick-

3

ness and duration, or it cannot exist. Matter, in other words, persists in time and space. Let me give you another illustration of this blending. How would you define motion?"

Again there was a dubious silence.

"Motion," said George suddenly, "why, that's when something—something material changes place." He was blushing at his own temerity; and he sat back in his leather chair, smoking furiously. He was a youth of no more than twenty.

"Quite so," smiled Rogers. "That, gentlemen, is about the way we all conceive motion. Something material, a railroad train, for instance, changes its position in space." He regarded the men before him, and this time there was a touch of triumph in his manner. "But, my friends, that's where our line of reasoning is inadequate. Time is involved equally with space. The train was there *then;* it is here *now*. That involves time."

"In other words—" the Doctor began.

"In other words, motion is the simultaneous change of the position of matter in time and space. You see how impossible it is to speak of one of the

4

factors without involving the others? That is the mental attitude into which I'm trying to get you. I want you to think of time exactly as you think of length, breadth and thickness — as one of the properties of space. Isn't that clear?"

The Big Business Man answered him. "I think so. I can understand now what you mean by a blending of —"

"Oh, his words are clear enough," the Banker interjected testily. "But what's the argument about? He started in by saying —"

George sat up sudden. "Mr. Rogers, you said we were to come here for something vitally important to you. Something about time and space. You said —"

Rogers interrupted him. "I did indeed. I asked you all to come here to the club to-night because you are my friends. Mine and Loto's. And the affair concerns him more directly than it does me."

He glanced across the room. "Come, Loto. You can't hide there forever, lad. You're the one to tell them."

The Chemist's son, a young man of twenty, rose

reluctantly from his obscure seat in a corner of the room. He was tall, and slight of build, with thick, wavy chestnut hair and blue eyes. His complexion was pink and white, with an overlying coat of tan. His features were delicate, almost girlish of mold, saved by a square firmness of chin. He came forward deprecatingly, flushing as the eyes of the men were turned on him—a graceful, poetic looking boy, with only the firm line of his lips and the set of his jaw to mark him for a man.

"My son, gentlemen," Rogers added. "You all know Loto."

"We do," said George enthusiastically. He vacated his own chair, shoving it forward, and selected another, more retired position for himself.

Loto sat down, his quiet gaze turning to Rogers. "Shall I tell them now, father?"

"Yes, lad, why not?"

The young man hesitated, as though in doubt how to begin. To one regarding him closely there would have been at once apparent a curious—almost abnormal—maturity mingled with his adolescence. He was still flushing, and yet his manner was thor-

6

oughly poised. His forehead was wrinkled in thought.

"Father and I were experimenting," he began abruptly, "about two years ago. We were interested in electrons. We were experimenting with the fluorescence in a Crookes tube — breaking down the atoms into electrons. Then we followed the experiments of Lenard and Roentgen. We darkened the tube and prepared a chemical screen, which grew luminous."

Loto turned to Rogers again: "They don't want to hear all this, father. These technicalities — "

Rogers smiled. "We hit upon it quite by accident — an accident that we have never been able to duplicate. We had, that evening, an adaptation of the familiar Crookes tube. I do not know the exact conditions we secured — we had no idea we were on the threshold of any discovery and we kept no record of what we did. Nor am I sure just how I prepared the screen — what proportions of the chemicals I used — "

"You're worse than Loto," the Banker growled. "If you'll just tell us what — "

7

"I will," agreed Rogers good-naturedly. "It was night—nearly midnight—in my laboratory on Forty-third Street only a few hundred yards from the Scientific Club here. The room was dark. We had set up a small chemical screen. It grew luminous as the electrons from the tube struck it; but the glowing was not what we had expected—not what we had observed before. The difference is unexplainable to you, but we both noticed it. And then Loto noticed something else—something in the darkness behind the screen."

Loto was sitting upright on the edge of his chair; his eyes were snapping with eagerness as he interrupted his father.

"I'll tell them because it was I who saw it first. Behind the screen the darkness of the room itself was growing luminous—a glowing radiance that seemed to spread out with rays that were not parallel, but divergent. It looked almost as though the screen were a searchlight sending a spreading beam out behind it.

"Father saw it almost as soon as I did. It was a very curious light; it did not illuminate the room

8

about us. Then we suddenly discovered that it went through the walls of the laboratory. We were looking into a space that seemed opening up for miles ahead of us. The walls of the room, the house itself, the city around us, were all blotted out. We were looking into an empty distance."

"Empty?" echoed George tensely. "Didn't you see anything?"

"Not at first." Loto had relaxed; his earnest gaze passed from one to the other of the intent faces of the men. "We were only conscious of empty distance. It was not darkness nor was it light. It was more a dim phosphorescence. We had forgotten the Crookes tube, the screen, everything but that glowing, empty scene before us.

"After a moment, or it may have been much longer, the scene seemed to brighten. It turned to gleaming silver, and then we saw that we were looking out over a snow-covered waste. Miles of it. Snow, back to the horizon, and a dull gray sky overhead. The ground seemed about sixty feet below us; we were poised in the air above it. Am I telling it right, father?"

"Yes," said Rogers. "You understand, gentlemen, that my laboratory is not on the ground floor of the building, but somewhat above the level of that part of the city."

"But—" began the Big Business Man.

"Let him go on," growled the Banker. "Go on, boy. Didn't you see anything but snow?"

"No, sir, not at once. It was all bleak and desolate. But it kept on brightening—losing its silver, glowing look until at last we could see it was daylight. It was apparently late afternoon—or perhaps early morning. The sun did not show—it must have been behind the gray masses of cloud.

"We sat staring down at this cold, snowy landscape—and then, almost from below us, something moving came into view. It had passed under us—under the laboratory—and was traveling on away from us."

"What was it?" the Banker demanded.

"A sled, sir. It seemed to be a huge sled, with fur covered figures on it, and pulled by an animal almost as large as a horse. But it wasn't a horse—it was a dog."

Loto paused; but no one else spoke. After a moment he resumed:

"The sled slackened and stopped—I suppose about a quarter of a mile from us. To the north—up toward where Central Park is now. And then we saw that there was a building there. It was white. It may have been of snow, or ice—or perhaps some whitish stone. It was low and oval, and quite large. There seemed to be an inclosed space behind it. The whole thing blended into the landscape so that we had overlooked it before.

"The sled stopped. We could see the figures climbing down from it. Then there came sudden darkness. The scene went black. We were sitting facing the side wall of the laboratory.

"A wire in our apparatus had burned out," Rogers explained. "And that night I was taken sick. It developed into typhoid and I was laid up for weeks. Loto was left alone to follow up our discovery."

"Just a minute," the Banker interjected. "Do I understand you to imply that you actually saw all this? It was not a vision, or an electrical picture or something, that you were reproducing?"

"No, they mean it was an actual scene," the Big Business Man put in. "They were seeing New York City of some other time. Isn't that so?"

Rogers nodded. "Exactly. And while I was sick, Loto went ahead and—"

"Was it the past?" the Doctor interposed. "You were looking back into the past?"

"We were looking across countless centuries into the future," said Loto.

"The future!"

"Yes," declared Rogers. "Must you always think of the future as a wonderful civilization of marvelous inventions—and mammoth buildings—and aeroplanes like ocean steamships? All that lies ahead of us no doubt. A hundred years—two hundred— a thousand—will bring all that. But further on? What about then, gentlemen? Ten thousand years from now? Or fifty thousand? Do you anticipate that civilization will always climb steadily upward? You are wrong. There must be a peak, and then a down grade—the decadence of mankind."

"Father, let me go on," Loto said eagerly. "I need not tell you all now exactly how we knew we were looking into the future and not the past. We did not know it that first evening. But later, when I studied the scene more closely, I could tell easily."

"How?" the Banker demanded.

"By the details I saw. The type of the building. That animal that looked like a dog. The sun — I'll tell you about that in a moment. An artificial light in the house — I saw it once or twice when it was night there. And the — the girl. Her manner of dress — "

"There was a girl?" said George quickly. "A girl! Tell us about her, Loto. Was she pretty? Was she — "

"Go on, boy," growled the Banker. "Tell it from where you left off."

"Yes, she was very pretty," said Loto gravely. "She — " He stopped suddenly, his gaze drifting off into distance.

"Oh!" breathed George; but at the Banker's glare he sat back, abashed.

Loto went on after a moment: "I won't go into details now. While father was sick I was able to examine the scene many times. I even think I —

13

well, I sat watching it most of the time for a week at least.

"The house had a sort of stable — or a kennel, if you want to call it that — behind it. And there was an open space, like a garden, with a wall around it. There was a little tree in the garden — a tree all covered with snow. But after a few days the sun came out and melted the snow on the tree branches.

"The girl was a captive. I guess they were bringing her in on that sled the night father and I first saw it. There was another woman about the place, and an old man. And a younger man — the one who was holding the girl a prisoner."

"You said the house looked about a quarter of a mile away," the Banker declared. "How could you see all these details?"

"I had a small telescope, sir."

"The scene actually was there," Rogers put in. "Loto used a telescope quite as he would have used one through the window to see Central Park. Go on, Loto."

"The girl — " George prompted.

"She was a small girl. Very slender — about six-

14

teen, I guess. She had long, golden hair — light golden, but it was red when she stood outside with the sun on it. That's because the sun was red — an enormous glowing red ball, like the end of a cigar. It tinged the snow with blood — but there didn't seem to be much heat from it.

" Sometimes I could see the girl through the doorway. There was a door, but it was transparent — glass, perhaps — and the house was lighted inside. She would sit on a low seat, with her hair in sort of braids down over her shoulders. Once she played on some little stringed instrument. And sang. I could see her so plainly it seemed curious not to hear her voice.

" They appeared to treat her kindly, even though she was a captive. But once the man came in and — and tried to kiss her. She fended him off. Then he went out and got on his sled and drove away. He was gone several hours.

" The girl cried that night. She cried for a long time. Once she ran outside, but one of those huge dogs came leaping out of the other building and drove her back. The dog's baying must have aroused

15

the place. The old man and the woman appeared; and they locked the girl up in some other room. I never saw her again.

"A week or two went by and father was better. But the next time I went to the laboratory, the apparatus wouldn't work. Perhaps the chemicals on the screen were worn out. Father doesn't know, and I don't. But we've never been able since to make a screen that would do more than glow. We've never had another that would affect the Time-space behind it."

"You mean," said the Big Business Man softly, "that after those brief glimpses into the future, it is closed again to you?"

Rogers spoke. "Tell them the rest, Loto."

The young man was flushing again. "Perhaps you gentlemen wouldn't understand. We have seen nothing more, but I — I couldn't forget that girl. I couldn't — give her up."

"*I* understand," George murmured. But Loto went on unheeding:

"It wasn't the scientific part of our discovery that impressed me most. Father kept that secret because we had no proof of what we had done — and we couldn't seem to get any. It was the girl that bothered me. That girl — a captive — facing some danger, I could only guess what. You gentlemen will say she isn't living — that she won't be alive for thousands of years yet. But *I* say your conception of it is wrong."

Loto's voice had gained sudden power. His manner had been ingenuous, almost naïve, but now youth dropped from him. He seemed abruptly years older — forceful, commanding.

"*You* say that girl *will be* living in the future. I say she *is* living in the future. She is living just as you and I are living — right here in this exact space that we call New York — within a few hundred yards of this room. She is separated from us, not by space, but only by time.

"You gentlemen perhaps cannot conceive of crossing that time. But if it were a mile of space — or a thousand miles — you could imagine crossing it very easily. Yet we know that time is a property of space — not one iota different from length, breadth and thickness except that we think of it differently."

17

Loto's flashing eyes held his little audience. "Gentlemen, suppose you — with your human intelligence — were a tree, rooted to one spot here in America. And suppose that the accustomed order of things was that Asia would come slowly and steadily toward you and pass before you. That is what time does for us. Do you suppose, under those circumstances, that you could readily conceive of going across space and reaching Asia? Think about that, gentlemen! It's easy for us to imagine moving through space, because we've always done it. But a tree with your intelligence would not feel that way about it. The tree would say: 'Asia *will be* here.' And if you said: 'That's true. But Asia exists just the same — in a different part of space from you. If you go there, you will not have to wait for it to come to you,' the tree — even if it had your present intelligence in every other way — wouldn't understand that. Simply because the tree had always conceived space as we are accustomed to conceive time. That conception of ours does not fit the real facts, for except for the way space and time affect us personally — there is actually no distinction to be made between them. That is no original theory of mine, or father's. It is modern scientific thought — mathematically proved and accepted ever since Albert Einstein first made his theory public."

A silence followed Loto's outburst. Rogers broke it.

"We would like to have you gentlemen meet us here two weeks from to-night. We are not quite ready yet. Will you do that?"

Every one in the room signified assent.

"But what for?" George asked earnestly. "Of course we will, but — has Loto discovered anything? Has he —"

Loto interrupted him. "I have been working — experimenting for two years." He had fallen back to his quiet manner. "Father has helped me, of course. And given me money — more than he could afford."

He smiled at Rogers, who returned it with a gaze of affection.

"In two weeks I will be completely ready. Don't you think so, father?"

"Yes," said Rogers; and a sudden cloud of anxiety

crossed his face. He was a scientist; but he was a father as well, and even his scientific enthusiasm could not allay the fear for his son that was in his heart.

"Yes," he repeated. "I think you will be quite ready, Loto."

"Ready for what?" growled the Banker. He was mopping his forehead with a huge white handkerchief.

Loto's glance swept all the men in the room. "I have found a way to cross time, just as you are able to cross space. And two weeks from to-night, gentlemen, with your assistance, I propose to start forward through the centuries that lie ahead of us. I'm going to find that girl — if I can — and release her — help her out of whatever danger — whatever trouble she is in!"

CHAPTER II.

INTO THE UNKNOWN.

"Honor to Loto," cried the Big Business Man. "The youngest and greatest scientist of all time!"

"There's a double meaning in that," laughed the Doctor, amid the applause. "The greatest scientist of time! He is, indeed."

It was outwardly a gay little gathering, having dinner in a small private room of the Scientific Club in the West Forties of New York City. But underneath the laughter there was a note of tenseness; and two of the people — a man and a woman — laughed infrequently with gayety that was forced.

The man was Rogers; the woman, Lylda, his wife, mother of Loto. She was the only woman in the room. At first glance she would have seemed no more than thirty-five, though in reality she was several years older — a small, slender figure in a simple black evening dress that covered her shoul-

21

ders, but left her throat bare. Her beauty was of a curious type. Her face was oval, her features delicately molded and of pronounced Grecian cast. Yet there seemed on her also an indefinable look of a woman of the Orient—her eyes, perhaps, which were slate gray, large and very slightly upturned at the corners, with long, very dark lashes. Her complexion was milk-white and rose, her skin smooth as satin. Her hair was thick, wavy and coal black.

No one could have said to what race Lylda might belong; but that she was a woman of intellect, culture and refinement was obvious. There was about her, too, an inherent look of tenderness—a gentle sweetness which in a woman and a mother could be nothing less than charming. Her eyes, as she met those of her men friends around her, were direct and honest. But when she regarded Loto this evening, a yearning melancholy sprang into them, with a mistiness as though the tears were restrained only by an effort.

The laughter about the table died out; a waiter was removing the last of the dishes; the men were lighting their cigars.

22

"Well," said the Banker out of a silence, "now let us hear it. If every one is as curious as I am —"

"More," put in George. "I'm more curious."

"You're right," agreed Rogers. "We must get on."

"First," the Big Business Man interrupted, "I want to know more about that screen behind which you saw that other time world of the future."

"I know very little myself," Rogers answered. "So little that Loto and I could never duplicate it. But the theory is understandable. The space where Central Park now is has a certain time factor allied to its other properties. The light, the rays, from that screen, whatever may have been their character, altered the time factor of that space.

"As Loto told you, the modern conception of the reality of things is that the future exists — but with a different time dimension. We have a familiar axiom, 'No two masses of matter can occupy the same space — *at the same time.*' That is just another way of saying it. To reason logically from that, an infinite number of masses of matter can, and do, occupy the same space — *at different times.*"

23

"I'd rather hear about this new experiment," the Banker said. "You made the statement—"

"So would I," agreed George. "That girl—"

"You shall," said Rogers. His grave, troubled glance went to his wife's face, but she smiled at him bravely. "You shall have all the facts as briefly as I can give them to you.

"Loto became obsessed—I can hardly call it anything less—with the idea that he could alter the time factor of human consciousness. In theory it was perfectly possible—I had to admit that. And so I let him go ahead. He has worked feverishly, with an energy I feared would injure his health, for nearly two years. But—gentlemen, this is all that counts—he has succeeded. I'm sure of that; he and I have already made a test. The apparatus is ready —upstairs now—and—"

"Let Loto tell it," grumbled the Banker. "Go on, boy, can't you tell us how you did it?"

"Yes, sir. I can in principle." Loto hesitated, then added with a quaint mixture of sarcasm and deference: "I can explain it to you in a general way, but the details are—very technical."

24

He paused until the waiter had left the room; then he began speaking slowly, evidently choosing his words with the utmost care.

"Matter, as we know it now, has four dimensions —the three so-called planes of space, and one of time. But what is matter? The new science tells us it is molecules, composed of atoms. And atoms? An atom is a ring of electrons—which are particles of negative, disembodied electricity, revolving at enormously high speeds around a central nucleus. Am I clear?"

Loto's gaze rested on the Banker, who nodded somewhat dubiously.

"Then," Loto went on, "we have resolved all matter to one common entity—that central nucleus of positive electricity which is sometimes called the proton. All this is now generally known and accepted. But of what substance—what character— is the proton? As long ago as 1923, or perhaps even before that, the theory was fairly accepted that the proton is merely a vortex, or whirlpool. And the electron was conceived to be something very similar. Do you grasp the significance of that? It robs matter of what I personally always instinctively feel is its chief characteristic — substance. We delve into matter — resolving its complexities to find one basic substance — and we find, not substance but a whirlpool — electrical, doubtless — in space!"

"That — makes you rather gasp!" the Big Business Man exclaimed, gazing about the table.

"It is quite correct," affirmed Rogers. "It transforms our conception of substance to motion. Of what? Motion of something intangible — the ether, let us say. Or space itself."

"I can't seem to get a mental grip on it," the Big Business Man declared. "You—"

"Think of it this way," Rogers went on earnestly. "Motion can easily change our impression of solidity. This is not an analogous case, perhaps, but it will give you something to think about. Water is normally a fluid. You can pass your hand through a stream of water from a garden hose. But set that water in more rapid motion, and what physical impression do you get? At Fully, Switzerland, water for a turbine emerges from a nozzle at a speed of four hundred miles per hour. What would happen if you tried to pass your hand through that? I have seen a jet no more than three inches in diameter of such rapidly moving water, and you cannot cut through it with the blow of a crowbar! There you have a physical substance — an impression of solidity — derived from motion."

"But what has all this to do with time?" the Banker objected, after a moment of silence.

"Everything, sir," said Loto quickly. "Since we are changing the time-dimension of matter, without altering its space-dimensions, you must have some conception of what matter really is. When once you realize the real intangibility of even our own bodies — or this house we are in — you will be able to understand us better."

The Banker relaxed. "Go on, boy; let's hear it."

"Yes, sir. Changing the time-dimension of substance amounts merely to a change in the rate and character of the motion that constitutes the electrical vortex we call a proton."

Loto looked at Rogers somewhat helplessly, with a faint quizzical smile twitching at his lips.

"I seem to talk very ponderously, father. I don't

mean to. I wonder if it wouldn't be easier for us to show them the apparatus?"

Rogers rose from his chair. "By all means. Gentlemen, Loto has completed his apparatus on the roof of the club here. You may have noticed for the past month that one end is boarded in, and has a canvas roof over it. That is where Loto has been working. Will you come up with us?"

The building that houses the New York Scientific Club is a full block in depth and twenty stories high. Its flat roof is surrounded by a parapet of stone. One end of the roof is a garden, with pergolas, trellised vines and flowers, and beds of flowers with white gravel walks between. At the other end, on this particular evening, a twenty-foot rough board wall enclosed a space about a hundred feet square, with a canvas roof above it.

The night was calm and moonless, with a purple sky brilliantly studded with stars. At this height the hum of the great city was stilled. A hush seemed in the air. Near by, many buildings towered still higher, but for the most part the roofs lay below — with their chimneys and pot-bellied water tanks set upon spindly legs like huge, grotesque bugs on guard. A block away a great hotel blazed with a roof garden of red and green lights. Spots of light crawled through the streets below, with black blobs that were pedestrians scurrying between them. Occasionally the drone of an aerial motor overhead broke the stillness.

Rogers led his four men friends across the roof top, and unlocked a tiny door that gave into the temporary board enclosure. Lylda and Loto entered last, the woman clinging to her son's hand. The turn of a switch flooded the place with light.

At first glance one would have said it was a modern passenger aeroplane that was standing there under the canvas — a huge, glistening dragonfly of aluminum color — a long, narrow streamline cabin below, the size of a small Pullman car, with windows of glass; a triplane above, flexible-tipped, and twin propellers behind, with four small horizontal ones on top.

"There," said Rogers, "is the product of Loto's work. What you see from here is merely an adaptation of the Frazia plane — and the Frazia Company built it for us. The apparatus flies as any other Frazia plane does. It has the same motors, the same equipment. Its other mechanism — by which the time-dimension, the basic electrical nature of the whole apparatus, and everything or everybody within its cabin can be changed at will — that mechanism Loto constructed and installed himself."

"There you go again," growled the Banker. "Let Loto tell it, won't you?"

Rogers bridled a little. "I'll tell you this, Donald. That is the apparatus in which Loto is going to cross time into the future. At least you can understand that — if you keep your mind on it."

There was a general laugh at the Banker's expense. But Lylda did not laugh. She was leaning against a wooden post, clinging to her son's hand, and staring at that sleek, shining thing with wide, terrified eyes.

"Come, Loto," said Rogers. "They want you to show it to them."

The young man disengaged himself from his mother and went forward. In a moment the men were scattered about, examining the plane.

"You may not understand the Frazia model," Loto was saying. "It was only put on the market recently. It is slightly larger than the average of the older types — more stable in the air — but no faster. It differs from the old styles chiefly in its employment of the helicopter principle for taking off and landing."

The Doctor had been stretching up to peer into one of the cabin windows; he turned to Loto.

"Just what is the helicopter principle?" he asked.

"The employment of horizontal propellers. They lift the machine straight up vertically into the air. As you know, the main defect of an aeroplane ten years ago was the necessity for a broad level space from which to start and on which to land. A horizontal velocity of some forty to seventy miles an hour was necessary before taking the air. And on landing the ground was struck at the same speed.

"The Frazia model changes all that. The horizontal propellers lift it straight up from the ground. At a height, say, of two or three thousand feet, these horizontal propellers are stopped, and by a very ingenious device they are folded up to be out of the

31

way. The machine, released from their support, drops downward, and after a few hundred feet begins to glide. Thus the forward velocity is attained. The vertical propellers are started and the flight proceeds as in the older models."

The Big Business Man had joined them. "I've read about the Frazias—they're advertising extensively. And in landing?"

"In landing, if a level space is available, the helicopters are not used. If not, the vertical propellers are shut off—at a considerable altitude—and the machine put into a spiral. The helicopters are opened slowly, and when they begin revolving they pick up the weight of the machine, allowing it to float downward at the will of the operator. In a strong wind this type of landing is not satisfactory, but if danger threatens below the plane may be raised and lowered again at some other place. It is not yet perfect, but it is a big improvement over the older forms."

The Banker called to them. He was standing on a box, looking into one of the windows. "You've got different rooms in here."

"Yes, sir," said Loto. "I've divided it into three small compartments according to my own needs."

"Can we get inside?"

"I think perhaps it would be better not to," said Rogers, coming forward. "At least, not to-night. Loto wants to get started. There is—"

"You plan to operate this—to-night?" the Doctor asked.

"Yes," answered Loto. "I am going forward in time, to—"

"To find that girl," George finished eagerly. "To rescue her. Don't you remember he saw her in that—"

"Be quiet, boy," the Banker commanded. "Loto, what is this other mechanism your father mentioned?"

"It is not particularly complicated," the young man answered readily. "In general principle, that is. The Frazia mechanism which I have explained causes the machine to travel through space—to change its space-factors at the will of the operator. That's clear, isn't it?"

"Of course it is," said the Banker impatiently.

"It's clear because you've always been able to travel through space yourself," interjected the Big Business Man. "Don't be so self-satisfied, Donald. If you'd been rooted to one spot all your life — like a tree — you wouldn't have a chance on earth of understanding an aeroplane."

"That's what I mean exactly," said Loto quickly. "My other mechanism changes the time-factor of the entire apparatus. I can explain it best this way: Every particle of matter in that machine—and my own body in its cabin — is electrical in its basic nature. My mechanism circulates a current through every particle of that matter. Not an electrical current, but something closely allied to it. The nature of this father and I do not yet know. But it causes the inherent vibratory movements of the protons of matter to change their character. The matter changes its state. It acquires a different time-factor, in other words."

"Is this change instantaneous?" the Doctor asked.

"No, sir. It is progressive. To reach the time-factor of to-morrow night, take the first few minutes of time as it seems to us to pass. The time-factor of next week would be reached during the succeeding two or three minutes."

"In other words, it picks up speed," said the Big Business Man.

"Yes. How long the acceleration will last I do not know. I have a series of dials for registering the time-movement. By altering the strength — the intensity — of the current, I can vary the speed, or check it entirely."

"But why have this apparatus in the form of an aeroplane?" asked the Banker. "You're going through time, not space."

Rogers answered: "In a hundred years from now this building will not be here. If we were to stop his time-movement at that point, he would drop twenty stories through space to the ground."

"Why, of course!" exclaimed the Big Business Man. "But in the air—"

"Exactly," said Loto. "I shall not start the propellers until later — until I am launched into future time, and need them."

Rogers looked at his watch. "Have you much to do before you start, Loto?"

"No, sir — nothing. I have food and water, clothing, and everything else I need. I filled our list very carefully, and checked over everything this afternoon. I could have started then; I've left nothing to do to-night."

"Then you might as well get away at once. You'll remember everything I've told you, Loto? You'll come back here, as quickly as possible? Here to this rooftop?"

The strain of anxiety under which Rogers was subconsciously laboring came out suddenly in his voice. "You'll be careful, lad?"

"Yes, sir — of course. I — well, I might as well say good-by now, father."

They shook hands silently, and Rogers abruptly turned away.

Loto shook hands with the others.

"I say, Loto, you'll bring that girl back, won't you?" George asked anxiously. "I want to meet her. Tell her I said that, will you?"

"Yes," said Loto gravely. "If I find her, I will, George."

The Banker had withdrawn to the farthest corner

of the inclosure, where he stood regarding the aeroplane fearfully. Loto went to him.

"Good-by, sir."

"Good-by, boy." The Banker's voice was gruff and a trifle unsteady. "Take it easy. Don't be a reckless fool just because you're young."

"No, sir; I won't."

Loto met his mother a few paces away. He stood head and shoulders above her, and her arms went around him hungrily as he bent down to kiss her.

"You'll come back to me, little son?" she whispered. "You'll come back — safely?"

"Yes, mother. Of course."

He met her eyes, with the terror lurking in their gray depths.

"Don't look like that, *mamita*. I'll be all right, of course."

Rogers was calling to them. With the thoughtlessness of youth Loto disengaged himself hurriedly.

"Good-by, *mamita*. I'll be back to-morrow or the next day. Don't worry — it's nothing."

He left her.

The last preparations took no more than a moment or two. Loto climbed to the cabin and disappeared within it.

"Be sure and take off the canvas roof later tonight," he called down to them. "And leave it off so I can get back."

"Yes," said Rogers, "we will. And one of us, at least, will be here watching all the time you're away. Good-by, Loto."

"Good-by, sir." The cabin door closed upon him.

At a distance of twenty feet the men stood in a little group, watching, wide-eyed and with pounding hearts.

"What will it look like going?" George whispered.

But no one answered him.

Presently a low hum became audible. It grew in intensity, until it sounded like the droning of a thousand winged insects. The aeroplane rocked gently on its foundation. It was straining, trembling in every fiber. The droning increased — a hum that seemed to penetrate not only the air, but the very marrow of the men who were listening to it.

A moment passed. Then the plane began to glow

— seemingly phosphorescent even in the light of the electric bulbs on the scaffolding beside it. Another moment. There was a fleeting impression that the thing was growing translucent — transparent — vapory. For one brief instant the vision and sound of it persisted — then it was gone!

The men stood facing a silent, empty space, where a few loose boards were lying, with a discarded hammer, a saw, and a keg of nails.

"Oh," murmured George at last. "It isn't there. It's — it's disappeared!" And then: "I do hope he finds that girl and brings her back. I want to meet her."

They had forgotten the woman. In an opposite corner of the enclosure Lylda was seated alone, crying softly and miserably to herself.

CHAPTER III.

SIX THOUSAND YEARS IN A NIGHT.

G EORGE sat alone on a little bench in the roof garden of the Scientific Club. On the ground beside him, stretched on a broad leather cushion, Rogers lay asleep. It was well after midnight. There was hardly a breath of air stirring, and only a few fleecy clouds to hide the stars. In the east a flattened moon was rising.

George sat with his chin cupped in his hands, staring out over the lights and the roofs of the city. The growing moonlight gleamed on his soft white shirt and white flannel trousers.

Rogers stirred and sat up. "Oh, you're awake, George?"

"Yes. Go on to sleep. I'm good for nearly all night."

But Rogers rose, stretching. "What time is it?"

"Quarter of two. Go on to sleep, I tell you."

"I've had enough." The older man sat down on

the bench and lighted a cigar. "You'd better take a turn, George. You'll wear yourself out."

"I can't. I'm too excited. How long has he been gone now?"

Rogers calculated. "About twenty-eight hours."

"Do you think he'll get back to-night?"

"I don't know. Perhaps."

"I wonder what he's doing right now," George persisted after a silence.

Rogers did not answer.

"You don't think anything could have happened to him?"

"No. I—I hope not."

"I want him to bring that girl back with him," George said after another silence. "I want to meet her—awfully."

Rogers plucked a flower from the trellis beside them, breaking it in his fingers idly. "He may get back to-night. It was our idea that—"

He stopped abruptly, and simultaneously George gripped him by the arm. An aeroplane motor was drumming directly overhead!

The familiar, gleaming white triplane hung there,

seemingly motionless, only a few hundred feet above them. Its helicopters were revolving; it was preparing to descend.

"Thank God!" murmured Rogers fervently.

"But—where's the girl?" George protested. "There he is!" He leaped to his feet and ran through the garden toward the head of the stairway that led below. "He's here! I'll call 'em up! He's here!"

They came up hurriedly from their rooms below; the men, sleepy-eyed but excited; the woman with relief and happiness lighting her tired face.

The Frazia plane had settled in its place within the wooden enclosure when they arrived. Its cabin door opened; Loto appeared.

Rogers called instantly: "You're all right, Loto?"

"Yes, sir; I'm all right. Have I been away long?"

He swung to the ground and they crowded around him. His cheeks were haggard and smeared with dirt; but that was temporary. The startling change was in his expression. His mouth had taken on a different look—a firmer set to the lips—and his eyes were the eyes of a man who had seen too much.

He smiled wanly. "Well, I'm here. Where's mother? Is mother all right?"

Again Lylda was standing apart.

Loto pushed past the men, and the woman's arms opened and took him in.

"But—where's the girl?" George protested. "Didn't you bring her back with you, Loto?"

Loto turned, with his arm about his mother's shoulders. "I found her; but I couldn't bring her back—just yet. I'll tell you it all when I get rested. *Mamita,* I'm hungry. I want a bath and some supper."

In a secluded room of the club they waited impatiently while Loto finished his meal. Then, with his mother clinging to his hand, he yielded to George's eager, reiterated questions.

"Yes, I found her—in that house about a quarter of a mile north of here. She was—"

"Won't you *please* begin at the beginning?" the Banker interrupted.

"Yes, sir." Loto smiled. He looked more like himself now, but still there was that curious, somber, brooding look in his eyes. "I will. Of course."

He hesitated a moment, then began slowly and earnestly:

"It was all so strange, so extraordinary, that even though I was prepared for almost/anything I could not have guessed how remarkable it would be."

"You mean your sensations?" the Big Business Man put in.

"He means what he saw when he found the girl," George declared. "Don't you, Loto? That world of the future where you stopped to locate her —"

"Both," said Loto. "It was an experience that I find difficult to describe — to picture adequately to you —"

"You went half a mile from here in space," the Doctor suggested. "How far did you go in time?"

"My idea would be to let *him* tell it," commented the Banker caustically. "If you people had any idea how irritating it is to me —"

"That's reasonable enough," agreed the Doctor readily. "Tell us just what happened, Loto — in your own way."

"I closed the door of the cabin after me," Loto began again. "I was in the forward one of the three compartments. It's a room perhaps eight feet wide and a little longer — a one-third section of the entire cabin. It has curving side walls, concave inside; and its arched ceiling is about seven feet high. It has two windows of heavy plate glass facing forward. A wider window on each side, and there is a floor window also.

"In this compartment are the controls for the Frazia motors and the flying controls. The controls of my own mechanism are there also. They are simple — merely a switch to regulate the Proton current, as father and I call it — and a series of small dials for recording the time-change. These dials are geared, with one for days, another for days in multiples of ten, one for years, and others for years in multiples ten, hundreds, and thousands. But I can show you all this in the plane itself."

"I noticed it," said the Doctor. "I looked in through one of the side windows just before you started."

"Go on, boy," the Banker urged.

"Yes, sir. I took my seat behind the Frazia controls. I was not going to use them at once, because there was no immediate need to raise the plane into the air. But I wanted to be seated; I could not tell what the shock of starting might be."

"I thought you said you had made a test," the Big Business Man put in, ignoring the Banker's glare.

"We did; but only with a small model. The dials and switch were on the wall at my right hand. I moved the lever of the switch over to the first intensity."

There was a breathless stir among the men. Loto went on, still more slowly, with obvious careful thought to his words: "There was a low hum. The floor seemed to rock under me. The humming increased; it roared in my ears. Everything was vibrating, with an infinitely tiny, trembling quiver that penetrated into my body, into my bones, even coursed through my blood.

"I'm not making myself clear. They were swift sensations, I suppose lasting no more than a few seconds. I felt, as near as I can explain it, as though some force that holds my own body together, cell by cell, were being tampered with — as if, had the struggle continued, I might be shattered into a myriad tiny fragments, like a puff of exploded powder.

"The humming grew still louder; I have heard something like it in my ears just before fainting. I remember trying to stand up. A wild impulse to throw back the switch and stop the thing came to me; but I resisted it. Then I was conscious of a sensation of falling headlong—a dizzy, sickening reeling of the senses rather than the body.

"I lost consciousness—for only a moment or two, I think. I was sitting in my seat—uninjured. The humming was still in my ears, insistent. But it was not so loud as I had thought, and after a time I came to forget it almost entirely.

"My first impression now was that everything about me was glowing—radiating a light almost phosphorescent. I looked down at my knees; my clothes were glowing. I could no longer distinguish color; my hands and my shoes were the same—all that same glowing phosphorescence. It gave a sense of unreality to everything. And then I saw that everything *was* unreal. There seemed no substance. I could distinguish the side of the cabin through my hand; and beyond the cabin wall I could see the solidity of the board inclosure where the plane was resting. It was as though my body and the cabin interior were shimmering ghosts; nothing but the world outside was substance. But when I gripped my knee with my hand I felt solid enough.

"I have given you details of my sensations as I remember them now, but I do not suppose that more than a minute or two had elapsed since I had first pulled the switch. I glanced at the dial recording the passage of days but there was no movement.

"I stood up, conscious of a nausea and a strong feeling of lightheadedness. I peered through one of the side windows. Outside, everything looked at first glance as though I had not yet started. The board walls of the enclosure were clear, solid and as distinct as before.

"Then I saw George staring directly at me, and I could tell by the expression of his face that he was looking, not at the plane, but at an empty space where the plane had been. Over in the corner mother was sitting. I could see she was crying, and father was comforting her."

Loto turned and smiled gently at his mother, then went on:

"It was all as real outside as though I had been part of it myself — until I saw the others move across the enclosure. They were walking extremely fast; their gestures were rapid — two or three times more rapid than normal.

"For what seemed like five or ten minutes I stood there watching you all. It was like a moving picture being run too fast — and being constantly accelerated. I saw you roll back the canvas roof — with movements incredibly swift. Then you went scurrying out through the door — the last of you so fast that the figure blurred to my sight.

"I was left alone. For a while I sat there, a little dazed. There is a small clock on the side wall of the cabin. It might have been completely radium-painted, by the look of it at that moment, but even though it glowed as intangible as a ghost, I could make out the hands. I was sure they would be traveling through space at their accustomed speed and thus give me the time of the world I had left."

"Why, that's so!" George exclaimed. "*I* never

thought of that. Our measurement of time is nothing but the movement of clock hands over space, is it?"

Loto did not heed the interruption. "I had started at about ten minutes of ten. The clock now showed about five minutes after ten — I had been gone fifteen minutes. Above the enclosure, to the east, I saw the moon. It was about an hour up, I judged. Do you know what time it rose last night?"

"About ten minutes of one," said Rogers.

Loto nodded. "That gives us a basis to compute my starting acceleration. The moon an hour up would have made your time ten minutes of two — four hours after I started. I had passed through those first four hours in fifteen minutes!

"This was with my control at the weakest intensity of the current. There are twenty subdivisions of power. I pushed the handle around from one to the other of them quickly — pausing only an instant on each, and stopping at the tenth. There was no change of sensation except that the humming seemed to grow, not louder exactly, but more powerful — more penetrating. The interior of the cabin and my own body lost visible density in appearance. You had switched off the electric lights outside, but in the moonlight I could still see the board walls, not only through the windows, but through the metallic sides of the cabin.

"I was tingling all over; but the sensation, now that I was used to it, was pleasant rather than the reverse — a feeling of lightness, buoyancy and strength.

"With the power increased tenfold, the acceleration of time-movement was enormous. The movement of the rising moon became visible; the heavens were turning over, the stars progressing from point to point with ever increasing speed.

"About ten minutes after ten by the clock, the moon was near the zenith, and the sun rose an instant later. I was conscious of a flash of twilight, and the sun's disk shot up from the horizon. The world was plunged into daylight.

"From my position inside the enclosure I could see nothing outside but the sky and one or two of the tallest buildings near at hand. There was no visible movement of anything but the sun. You can understand that, of course. Had any of you come into the enclosure, or had an aeroplane passed overhead, I would not have seen either. The movement would have been too rapid for my vision.

"In perhaps a minute or two the sun was directly overhead, and in another fraction of a minute it had set. Darkness was upon me. Then the moon rose again and flashed across the heavens. Clouds formed and disappeared so quickly I could hardly see them.

"I glanced at the dial recording days. Its hand was moving. One day had passed, and the hand was traveling toward the next.

"For ten minutes or so I sat there, while day succeeded night, and night came again — only to be followed almost instantly by the daylight. Soon I could distinguish only thin streaks of light as the sun and moon crossed above me — streaks that came closer together, merged into one, and separated again as the month passed. And then the days became so brief that they blurred with the nights. A grayness settled upon everything — the mingled twilight of light and darkness.

"The hand of the day dial was sweeping around swiftly. I looked at the dial beside it, which recorded days in multiples of ten. Its pointer was also moving. Forty odd days were recorded and the movement was accelerating every instant."

Loto paused. "Have you any questions?"

"No," growled the Banker. Beads of moisture stood out on his thin, blue-veined forehead. "No questions. Go on, boy."

"I thought then I had better leave the rooftop," Loto continued with his same slow voice. "I started the Frazia helicopters, and rose about a thousand feet. Then I slowed them down until a balance with gravity was maintained, and I hung stationary. You gentlemen, if you think of it at all, may be surprised that the flying mechanism was effective while I was sweeping so swiftly through time. If our atmosphere did not persist in time, the propellers would have exerted no pressure against it. But the air does persist, and so does gravity.

"There was apparently no wind. The transient winds and storms of a few hours were all blended. The result, however, must have been a slight in-

53

fluence to the northward, for I found myself drifting very slowly in that direction. After a few moments my time-velocity had so increased that even that drift was averaged. I hung motionless.

"From this height — a thousand feet above the southern boundary of Central Park — the scene below me was a strange one. At first glance, I might have been hanging in a balloon, on a dull, soundless day very heavily overcast. Except that the sky, instead of showing dark clouds, was a queer, luminous gray blur that distinguished nothing.

"The city below me lay clear cut, but absolutely shadowless, which gave it a very extraordinary look of flatness — a vista of buildings painted upon a huge, concave canvas. There were colors distinguishable, but they were abnormally grayish and drab. Vague, unreal pencil points of light dotted the scene — electric lights that were on every night in the same spots, and off in the daytime — the blended effect of which was visible. There was no sound. I could not have heard it above that insistent humming, even had there been. But I knew there was not. Nor was there motion. It looked a dead, empty city. The streets seemed deserted — not even a blur to mark those millions of transitory movements of humans and vehicles that I knew were taking place.

"I had been conscious of a brief period of chill, and for a moment or two the scene had assumed a whiter aspect, especially in the park. I conceive this was from a blending of several heavy, lingering snowfalls of the winter.

"The lowest dial, marking days, now showed only a blur as its pointer swept around. And the year-dial pointer was visibly moving. I had passed one year and was well into the second. The clock showed ten thirty. I had been gone forty minutes!

"I said there was no visible movement in the scene beneath me. That was so, at first, but I soon began to see plenty of movement. The white look had come and passed again — far briefer this time — when my attention was caught by a building on Broadway, along in the Fifties somewhere. It was a broad but low building, no more than eight or ten stories high — the lowest in its immediate vicinity. It seemed now to be melting before my eyes! That is the only way I can describe it—melting. Parts of it were vanishing! It was dismembering, as though piece by piece unseen machinery and human hands were taking it apart and carrying it away. Which, gentlemen, is exactly what was happening.

"Can you form a mental picture of that? I hope so, for it was characteristic of all the movement that now began to assume visibility throughout the silent city. This building that melted—I come back to that word because it seems the only one suitable—was gone in a moment or two. Try to conceive that I did not see actual movement—not the physical movement we are accustomed to. They were tearing down that building—doubtless over a period of weeks. But I could not see any specific thing being done—any part of the building come off and move away. All such details were too rapid—far too rapid. What I saw, rather, was the *effect* of movement—a change of aspect—not the movement itself. The building progressively looked smaller—until at last it was not there.

"Then another building began rising in its place. It grew steadily. It was as if I were blinking, and between each blink, with an unseen movement, it had leaped upward another story. It seemed a skeleton at first, and then it was clothed. I watched it, ignoring others further away, until it stood complete — a full block in depth and thirty or forty stories high.

"I began to realize now the tremendous acceleration of time velocity I was undergoing — like a number that is not added to, but constantly doubled. The year-dial pointer very soon had moved to ten years; the pointer of the century-dial was stirring. Again I glanced at the clock. It was after eleven; I had been gone about an hour and a quarter.

"There was nothing that I had to do, and I moved about the cabin, looking out of each of the windows in turn. The city was rising — not one building, but hundreds. As my time velocity increased I could no longer see them come and go individually. They were there — and then they were gone, and others always larger and higher were in their stead.

"So I say the city was rising — coming up to meet me as I hung a thousand feet above it. Already one gigantic edifice to the south seemed to rear its spire above me. The edges of the island stayed low — a fringe of the new and the old mingled; but down the backbone, roughly following Broadway, great piles of steel and masonry were coming up.

"To the southeast I could make out the bridges over the river. There were others now — extraordinarily broad and high, dwarfing the older ones that stood neglected beside them.

"It was a period of tremendous activity. And suddenly I discovered that the southern half of Central Park was obliterated. I had drifted a little further north and was over it. A building was rising — coming up toward me so swiftly that its outlines were blurred and shadowy. I was gazing down through the plate glass floor window, and caught a vague impression of a network of gigantic steel girders almost underneath the machine.

"I was too low. I accelerated the helicopters and ascended perhaps another thousand feet. When I was again hanging stationary, I found beneath me a tremendous terraced building — a pyramid with its apex sliced off. To the north and south it connected with others of its kind — giant structures generally of pyramid shape, with streets running along their steplike terraces. Innumerable bridges connected these mammoth buildings, so that north and south, and for a few blocks east and west from the center, there were continuous aerial streets, as many as ten or fifteen, one above the other, in some places.

"I turned to the window facing the north. There was now nothing but buildings as far as my line of vision extended — buildings a thousand feet or more high, like a ridge down the center, shading off to the lower areas of the east and west. There were trees and parks in spots on the top, but the original ground was covered.

"The upper street levels — those alternate sections of terraces and bridges over courtyards whose ground was merely the rooftops of lower edifices — were some of them laid with gleaming rails. And rearing itself above everything, a skeleton structure of monorails stretched north and south — eight or ten single rails paralleled at widths of some fifty feet, which I realized must be carrying some system of aerial railroad.

"This towering pile was indeed the backbone of the city, extending roughly north and south like a mountain range that forms the backbone of a continent. The lower areas adjacent — five hundred feet above the ground, perhaps — were for the most part buildings with broad, flat roofs, with winding paths among which I could see trees springing up with visible growth.

"In Jersey, on Long Island, and north of Manhattan as far as I could see, lesser cities had appeared, with occasional giants among buildings that were lower. The whole was now welded into one, for the rivers on each side of me were spanned by a bridge at almost every street — a network of bridges under which the water flowed almost unnoticed.

"My time-velocity was still accelerating. I saw now, increasingly, many things about the city that were shadowy — structures that were erected and stood no more than twenty or thirty years, perhaps, which to my vision now was only a moment. I became aware, not only below me, but even above me, of occasional vague aerial structures — skeletons that reared themselves up a few thousand feet and dissipated into nothing before I could form a conception of their real nature.

60

"There was, indeed, everywhere this shadowy aspect as to detail. Changes were taking place; things were being done even the effect of which was too fleeting for my vision to grasp. Once, to the south, I saw a great yellow light. It may have lasted ten or twenty years. I cannot say. Its effulgence spread out horizontally for a hundred miles or more, and radiated up into the sky like a gigantic conflagration at night. A beacon light? Perhaps it was. It flared up and was blotted out in a moment.

"I was constantly losing more details, but in general the growth of the city was outward and upward. Presently there came a pause, as though the city were resting. Occasional areas were blurred by their changing form — across the river in Jersey a tremendous tower was rising into the sky far above me; but as a whole the scene had quieted. My brain was confused by what I had tried to observe and comprehend. I found myself hungry and a little faint. I dropped into my seat.

"The dials beside me caught my attention. The century-dial pointer had passed eighteen. Eighteen hundred years, and approaching two thousand even as I sat staring at it! The clock marked one forty. I had been gone almost four hours!"

Loto paused to light himself a cigarette. His face was solemn; there was not a trace of youth left in his look or in his voice. "I see you want to question me. You shall, in a moment. I said the city was resting. That is true. The growth of two thousand years had carried it to what splendors of mechanical perfection I could only guess at. But now it seemed to have reached its height; the summit of human achievement — in the building of this particular city at any rate — had been attained.

"I waited and watched through another period. There were changes, but they were minor. I suppose all the buildings and various structures decayed and were replenished. I do not know. The changes were too fleeting for me to see — and the general form remained the same.

"I was at what seemed the pinnacle of civilization, where mankind was resting and enjoying the results of its labors. Decadence? It was bound to come, gentlemen — as truly as death followed birth. I could not realize it then, with all that evidence of

62

power and magnificence beneath me — just as I suppose those humans could not realize it themselves. But it was coming; and presently I was to see it come — stagnation, ruin and decay, where always before there had been achievement and advance.

"The clock now recorded two fifty. I had been gone five hours. The century-dial was beyond thirty-seven hundred years. Two thousand years of growth upward from our own time-world, and only two thousand more of resting on the summit before the inevitable decadence began. It is life, gentlemen. He who stands still, goes backward. And so it is with mankind as a whole. This triumphant city went down almost as quickly as it had come up. And through the windows of that cabin I watched it — neglected a little at first, then more and more as its softened masters, with nature turned against them, became unable to cope with it, until at last it broke up and sank back into ruin, decay and desolation."

CHAPTER IV.

THE GIRL CAPTIVE.

L OTO paused. "You had some questions?"
For a moment there was an awed silence among the men.

"It's almost too extraordinary to comment on," the Big Business Man murmured. His gaze drifted off into vacancy. "Just think — this city of ours, what a future it has! How small a part of its life — its history — we are!"

"That's exactly what strikes me," the Doctor exclaimed. "A lifetime of sixty or seventy years, which seems so important to each of us! What is it? Pouf! We are born, we live and we die. Our little individual achievements are nothing but an infinitesimal fraction of human progress."

"True," said Loto gravely. "But you must not forget that all progress is nothing but the sum of such little individual achievements."

"Your reaction is natural, Frank," put in Rogers.

" But to me, such thoughts only destroy egotism and strengthen ambition. We are none of us more indispensable than a single ant is to its colony; but out of our efforts — yours, mine, and all of those who live with us to-day — the world is carried on. The only individual who should feel small and unimportant is he who accomplishes nothing — who does not justify his existence."

"I hate abstract arguments," the Banker grumbled. "Loto's experience is something concrete. Why can't we —"

"I'd like to hear more about that light," George interposed eagerly. He turned to Loto. "You said it was a beacon light — that big yellow flare you saw to the south. You said maybe it lasted twenty or thirty years. Did you mean a signal — a huge light they had made to try and signal the inhabitants of some other planet?"

"I thought of that," the Big Business Man exclaimed. "Is that what you meant, Loto?"

"It was in my mind," Loto answered. "It might have been that — or any one of a thousand other things."

"I've been wondering," said the Big Business Man slowly, "how the future of our world would be influenced by the other planets. Some of them must be inhabited. Are they — those inhabitants of Venus, or Mars or Mercury — never coming here? Are we never going there?"

Lylda said, quietly, with the clear vision of prophecy on her face and in her voice: "That all will be, my friend. It is certain. We cannot remain long isolated on this earth — not so much longer than we have been up to now."

Loto smiled admiringly at his mother — a glance that his father instantly noted.

"Did you learn something of that, lad? You can tell us?"

"Yes, sir. Something of it. Our world here is not to remain long in isolation."

"You went to a time when people from another planet were here?" the Big Business Man demanded.

Loto shook his head. "No. They were not here. They had been here and gone."

A chorus of questions would have broken forth, but the Banker's voice rose above them.

"It seems to me we're not getting anywhere." His glare swept the men, and softened to a quizzical smile as it came to Lylda. "You, Mrs. Rogers, and your son, are the only people in the room — besides myself — who have any intelligence whatever. If they'd only listen, instead of talking so much —"

"Go on, Loto," Rogers said smilingly.

Loto hesitated, and his face grew solemn as his thoughts went back to what he had been describing.

"I was telling you about the city at its height. It was resting. For two thousand years, perhaps, it remained comparatively unchanged. Then, very little at first, I began to see evidences of its decadence. It was not that it grew smaller, but that parts of it as they decayed were not replenished.

"I think now that my acceleration of time-velocity had ceased; I was progressing forward at a uniform, or nearly uniform rate."

"What rate?" the Big Business Man demanded.

"I did not figure it very closely. I remember looking at the clock about this time. It was quarter after three. I had been gone nearly five and a half hours. The dials read forty-five hundred years."

"What rate would that be?" the Big Business Man persisted.

Loto smiled. "Perhaps you can figure it out. I should say that averaging it up — I had been steadily accelerating, you remember — that my maximum time-velocity was some fifteen hundred to two thousand years an hour."

"That time-velocity was carrying you forward through some twenty-five or thirty years a minute," the Doctor mused. "A lifetime every two minutes!"

"Yes, sir. I calculated it to be that. I found myself hungry. I ate a little and then went back to the window. My heart leaped into my throat. To the north there was a scene of destruction such as I had never conceived could be possible. The whole northern section of the city lay in ruins.

"Can you imagine what that looked like, gentlemen? Not the New York of to-day, as it would look battered down, but that later, gigantic city. Buildings a thousand feet high; towers twice that; aerial streets — twenty of them, one above the other; bridges solid across the rivers; and the whole over an area of several miles laid into a tumbling mass

68

—so monstrous that even its ruins covered the ground several hundred feet deep."

"You're not describing natural decay," the Big Business Man explained. "It was—some tremendous catastrophe?"

Loto's quiet gesture was affirmative. "Yes, sir, I think so. There had been evidences of decadence throughout the city. A building here and there broke down and was in ruins. That great system of monorails that bisected the city to the north and south and towered over everything had fallen apart and was left dangling.

"But this destruction that swept over the northern end was different. It must have come very quickly. I did not see it; I was away from the windows those few moments.

"A catastrophe? I conceived it to be that. It may have taken a day—or a century. But I think it came suddenly.

"Before I had opportunity to collect my thoughts, I was staring at a scene of *past* ruin—segments of broken buildings, ivy covered; piles of debris with trees growing in their midst. And as I watched, the vegetation spread, leaving only here and there a tumbling, decrepit, age-old wreck of what once had been an edifice."

"But what did it?" George demanded.

"It might have been an earthquake or something of the kind," the Doctor suggested.

Loto shook his head. "I don't think so. I should have seen evidences of that. No, it was, I think, destruction at the hand of man."

"War!" exclaimed the Big Business Man. "Five thousand years from now!"

Rogers nodded in quick agreement. "The last war will be between the two last mortals," he said, and smiled quizzically. "Loto, you have some idea what—who caused that catastrophe."

"Yes, sir. From what I learned later, I conceive it was the attack of inhabitants from another planet. You, *mamita,* said we are not long to remain in isolation on this earth. It is true. They will come from other planets—perhaps even now in our own lifetime."

Loto stopped for a moment, and George promptly supplied him with a cigarette. "Thanks. The history of our world, from almost the present on, is colored by our intercourse with the other planets. I think the City of New York — as I saw it rise to its peak of splendor — was built entirely by humans of our own earth. Perhaps elsewhere that was not so. That beacon light — it may have been to reestablish communication, which had begun centuries before. And this catastrophe — it was war I am sure — an attack from some other planet. It left the city apathetic; it was just that extra impetus which was needed to start it downhill.

"The northern section was never rebuilt. And the rest began to fall apart rapidly. Perhaps a large proportion of its inhabitants had been killed. Perhaps the invaders did not settle in it. I could not know such details. But I could see it all neglected. Bridges dangling; buildings fallen and left in ruins; areas melting away into the upspringing vegetation.

"Occasionally some brave effort was made to build on a different scale. There were other types of architecture — always smaller; little sections newly built stood heroically, surrounded by gigantic, moldy ruins in the midst of woods.

"Suddenly I realized that it was a dead city at which I was staring! There were now no changes except those natural to the passing years. The city was deserted; its inhabitants had died or had fled — or both.

"It was after five o'clock. The dials registered just short of eight thousand years."

Again there was a brief silence; then Loto went on as before.

"I had less to see now, and I could give my attention to other things. The ruins of a dead city do not remain long in visible existence. Two thousand years more were recorded. Beneath me the vegetation seemed untouched by the hand of man; only in a few scattered places were ruins — a tumbledown segment of building; the broken base of a tower; a skeleton of crumbling steel here and there; headstones on the grave of what once had been a city.

"With these changes the contour of the landscape itself was forced on my attention. The rivers had changed. They were broader. South of Manhattan Island, and somewhat to the west, I could distinguish a great expanse of water. All the lowlands there — the 'Meadows,' as we call them — had sunk. To the north the land seemed higher than normal, and an arm of the sea had crept in up there to lap the foothills.

"I have not told you of the temperature I was experiencing. When I started there was an almost immediate drop — a blending of day and night, winter and summer. It penetrated into the cabin — almost cold after the warm August evening of my departure.

"Now, however, at seven o'clock, when I had been gone some nine hours, I felt that it was growing noticeably colder. And the faintest suggestion of a vague whiteness began to creep into the scene below me. That is an odd way for me to phrase it, gentlemen, but it must serve. You must realize I was seeing each minute only the *effect* of the snowfalls of thirty winters — blended with all the other seasons. The snowfalls were increasing in severity; I became aware of that in the aspect of the scene — but I cannot describe it."

"How far had you gone then?" the Big Business Man interrupted.

73

"It was after seven o'clock. I had been gone about nine and a half hours. The dials showed eleven thousand four hundred and fifty odd years. I now faced a new problem. This landscape we had seen in our experiment — father and I — had nothing in it of great duration. How could I find it — tell when I had reached its time? That house in which the girl was held captive — it could stand no more than a hundred years, if that. And it was the only distinguishing mark in the whole scene. I would pass the lifetime of that house in a minute or two. I puzzled over this for quite a while. I had almost decided to stop and verify the actual, momentary conditions beneath me. And then I realized I still had far to go. There were trees, plenty of them, beneath me. They were constantly shifting and changing, but quite distinguishable, nevertheless. And in the enclosure about that house father and I had seen a tree — the only tree in the landscape. It was a curious looking tree — stunted, and with a look of the far north about it. These below me, at eleven and twelve thousand years ahead of our present, were more or less normal looking trees — or they

74

probably would have been had I stopped to examine them.

"I still had far to travel so I increased the current from the tenth to the fifteenth intensity. Again I was conscious of that feeling of lightness in my head —and the humming and vibration of everything increased. I had almost forgotten my personal sensations—had quite forgotten them, in fact, for several hours past.

"I passed fifteen thousand years. I could see that the ocean to the north had come further inland. There was now, from my altitude, no evidence of mankind visible—nor anything to indicate that man had ever lived on this earth. The scene was more blurred now—and grayer. I could still make out the bay to the south, with a range of hills on Staten Island and water behind it and to the west as far as I could see. The rivers bounding Manhattan were still there—the Palisades of the Hudson had broken down.

"Directly beneath me was forest. I believed I had not drifted much from my original position. I was still over where Central Park had been some twenty thousand years before. The forest—it was more a woods—covered a narrow rolling country between the two rivers. I knew I was moving through time much more swiftly now—perhaps twice as fast as before. The vegetation was blurred —almost distorted. It was changing constantly; and on the whole, was growing sparser, more stunted. It was as though I were traveling northward, or ascending a mountain almost to the timber line. Another interval passed. My time-velocity had so increased that once I thought I could see a hill rising—another area sinking. But that probably was imagination.

"I had been gone some twelve hours—it was almost ten o'clock—when I realized I was about exhausted. My head was reeling; my eyes burned and watered. It was growing much colder—so cold that I switched on the electrical heating apparatus.

"That was when the dials recorded between twenty and thirty thousand years. I don't remember exactly. I was confused. The scene beneath me was noticeably whiter, and I was now drifting to the south. I felt perturbed. I was going too far.

"I had reached about forty-five thousand years when abruptly I realized that there was no vegetation in the scene! Just when it melted away I had not noticed. It was all a whitish blur now, that suggested very snowy winters blended with a shorter summer season. I leaped to the control, and threw its handle back, pausing an instant at each intensity of current until I had come to the first. There I left it.

"These new sensations of decreasing my time-velocity so abruptly were almost equally as severe as those when I started. The humming slowed up. My whole body seemed turning to lead — or freezing. I was heavy, stiff, and cold. I was standing up, and I managed to grip the side of the cabin for support; and reaching down, I threw off the switch, cutting off the current completely. There came a tremendous, soundless clap in my head; I seemed tumbling headlong into an abyss of blackness.

"I do not think I lost consciousness," Loto continued. "My senses reeled for what seemed an age, but was doubtless only a second or two. I fell into a chair, with my face down in my crooked arm.

The horrible dizziness passed; I raised my head and looked about me.

"My first impression was of the extraordinary solidity of the cabin interior. I had not realized how shadowy it had been before. Two little electric bulbs were burning overhead. They illuminated the compartment. The windows were black rectangles; it was night outside.

"I was cold; I could see my breath in the chill of the room, even though one of the electric heaters was in operation. Everything close to me was oppressively silent; the humming still seemed to persist vaguely, but I knew it was only the reaction from it roaring in my ears. And from the next compartment came the drone from the Frazia helicopter motors.

"When I had fairly recovered normality, I went to the nearest window. The sky was blue-black. There was no moon; the stars seemed a trifle hazy. Beneath me I could make out a barren expanse of snow. I was blowing swiftly to the southward."

"How could you tell the direction?" the Big Business man interrupted. "You couldn't see any familiar conformation to that landscape at night, could you?"

"No, sir. But I had a compass. Its needle had steadied now, and I saw that my drift was almost directly south. I was alarmed. I knew that, even with the compass, I could easily get lost—geographically, so to speak.

"My first action was to increase the revolutions of the helicopters and ascend. When I was up some six thousand feet I shut them off, folded the helicopter propellers, and went into a glide. A moment more and I was flying—back northward, against the wind.

"I was hopelessly lost—both in time, and in space. I could distinguish nothing in the starlit, snowy landscape that seemed familiar. Whether or not I had passed the time world I was seeking, I had no idea.

"I flew low, skimming the snow no more than one or two hundred feet above it. There were houses! Huts would be a better word. I think they were built of snow—I could not tell. It seemed an Arctic world."

"You went too far. You passed the girl's world," George said eagerly.

"Yes. I decided to stay near there until morning. Fortunately that proved only a short time away. Within half an hour the East began to brighten. The stars paled; twilight came and passed, and the sun rose — a huge, red, glowing ball.

"I was circling about, quite high — six or eight thousand feet possibly. By this reddish light of early morning I could see the bay south of me. There was no Long Island; the ocean had closed in to the north and east, and I was near its shore — a cold, snowy beach, with lazy rollers. But west of me there was a river — the Hudson, I was sure — a river double the breadth of the one I had known. It seemed to come from a mountainous region in the northwest, and an arm of it north of Manhattan emptied into the sea.

"Everywhere was snow. The bay was full of floating ice. Across the river was an area of stunted trees. I was over Manhattan Island, I was sure. I circled around, searching. It was not the time world I was seeking — that was obvious. Should I go on

—or back through the centuries I had passed? I decided on the latter.

"I had now been away from you nearly sixteen hours. I was worn out. I flew across the river, found a level plateau to the north. There was no sign of human habitation in the vicinity. Shutting off my Frazia motors completely, I descended, and came to rest on the surface of the snow, in a time world forty-six thousand and eight years beyond our present. I ate a little, and dropping to the floor of the cabin, fell asleep."

"Wasn't that rather unwise?" the Doctor suggested. "Suppose some inhabitants of that time world had come upon you sleeping there?"

"Yes," Loto agreed. "But I had to take a chance. Even with the abnormally large reserve tanks of my Frazia plane, I had not enough petrol to run the motors more than a hundred hours. I could not afford to waste it."

He shrugged.

"At all events, I awakened without having been disturbed. It was night again. I had slept some twelve hours. I flew upward, back over Manhattan

Island — and threw the opposite Proton current into its first intensity.

"I need not go into further details, gentlemen. My sensations were the same as before, though they bothered me less, as I grew more accustomed to them. I came back through time. At intervals I would stop and examine the landscape.

"The wind was blowing almost continually from the north during all these centuries. But I was not using the helicopters, and I flew into it slowly, keeping my approximate position without great difficulty. I tried to hold myself near the south center of the island, and look northward. I was right in going back through time, I soon discovered. From close to the ground where I stopped once, I could see a rolling hill near by that had a familiar contour. I cannot describe it to you, gentlemen, but once I saw it from that angle, I knew it was in the landscape we had seen from the laboratory.

"Then I found the tree. There was no house. No snow, either, for I had chanced then to stop in a summer season. The tree was too small. I chose a ten years later time world, and watching the dials closely, descended at a ten and a half year later period. I had struck it exactly—within a week or two it must have been from the time world father and I had observed."

There was a stir among Loto's little audience. George sucked in his breath sharply.

"Oh! And then you—"

"I had occupied some eight hours with this search. The dials had stopped now at twenty-eight thousand two hundred odd years. I was at that instant flying at an altitude of no more than a few hundred feet. It was again early morning; just after sunrise—that familiar, snowy landscape father and I had seen from the laboratory.

"The house lay below me, with its enclosure and outbuildings; I circled over it, staring down through the floor window. The Frazia motors are greatly muffled, as you doubtless know, but even so, their sound carried down to the house. A figure came out into the enclosure, and stared upward at me. It was the girl—in a fur garment, but bareheaded—watching my plane. Before I could think what to do, three huge dogs—each of them the size of a pony—came leaping from one of the outbuildings and stood in a group, baying up at me with snarling voices of such volume and power that they made my blood run cold.

"I was circling slowly over the house, cursing my lack of caution and still too confused to do anything, when the figure of a man appeared in the enclosure—a man in furs and bareheaded like the girl. He stood head and shoulders over her. Evidently the noise of the dogs blotted out the sound of my motors. He did not look up into the air, but striding angrily to the girl, struck her with the flat of his hand full across the mouth. Then he dragged her cowering into the house."

CHAPTER V.

THE FIRST ENCOUNTER.

"I HAD straightened out, and was flying south. The howling of the dogs died away. Without realizing where I was going, I headed down the wind. Soon I was over the water. I had risen, and in the morning light could see the landlocked bay into which the main channel of the Hudson emptied; the bay itself had an entrance to the sea almost at the river's mouth.

"It was midwinter, I afterward learned. The river and the bay both seemed frozen over with a mantle of snow on their ice. I passed above an island — Staten Island, no doubt — and mechanically swung to the west.

"What was I to do? I had several rifles in the plane, as you know — and one of the latest Collinger hand guns. My instinct was to land at the house boldly, overawe its inmates with my weapons, and carry off the girl. That was a fatuous thought. I very soon realized that for all I knew they might have the power to strike me dead with some weapon totally unknown.

"I was still flying West. I found myself far out over Jersey, and still I had decided nothing. There were houses beneath me — even a little village or two — white, and blending with the landscape. But I did not heed them, though fortunately I had sense enough to ascend to a high altitude where I could escape observation.

"The sun was rising above the sea behind me, and at last I swung about to face it. As it mounted higher — it was moving at about normal speed — some of the red, glowing look was lost; it assumed more its familiar aspect of our own time world. But still an hour above the horizon as it was now, I could stare at it quite steadily without being blinded."

"I wanted to ask you about that sun," the Big Business Man began. "Is it your idea that the change of climate —"

"Not now," the Banker objected. "For Heaven's sake —"

"I was heading East," Loto resumed obediently.

"In another ten minutes I would have been back in Manhattan.

"Abruptly a course of action came to me. I would leave the plane secluded somewhere and approach the house on foot — quietly. If I could only elude the dogs — not arouse them — I hoped to be able to get into the house and get the girl out. Once I could get her outside and back to the plane. Yes, *mamita,* it was a foolhardy plan. I realize it now. I know I should not have risked such an attempt.

"I flew very low up the Hudson from its mouth. I was afraid I might be seen. Then it suddenly occurred to me how easily I could avoid that for a certainty. I threw the switch of the Proton current into the first and then the second intensity; and began a slow time flight forward through the day simultaneously with my flight up the river.

"I found a good hiding place for the plane, on the east bank of the river — a broad, flat sort of gully some two hundred feet wide — I figured this was about abreast of the house — and I lowered the plane into it with the helicopters. It was difficult to do because of my southward drift, but I managed

87

it. As I neared the ground I shut off the Proton current and came to rest in time and space almost together.

"The sun was just setting behind a line of hills across the river. I had not eaten for several hours; I sat in the cabin now and ate, planning exactly what I should do to rescue the girl.

"You will not understand it, gentlemen, but as I sat there alone, with no one to consult, it did not seem to me so desperate an enterprise. My Collinger — no bigger than your hand — would fire soundlessly and smokelessly a dozen bullets in as many seconds, each capable of killing a human, or one of those dogs.

"It was the dogs I was most afraid of. And yet — I had observed from the laboratory — they did not run loose about the grounds at night, but were trained to stay in the kennel, which was some distance from the dwelling. Three or four hundred feet, perhaps.

"I decided to start about midnight. My clock gave a totally different hour, of course, from the correct one of that particular time world. But I was planning to leave the plane about six hours after sunset.

"It was a long evening, but the time finally arrived. I put on my fur coat—one with the fur outside—and went bareheaded. Why? Because I wanted to look as rational to the girl as possible. She would be afraid of me at best—a stranger—doubtless more afraid of me than of her captors. I realized fully what a difficulty that would be. An outcry from her—resistance on her part—might lose me everything."

"Wouldn't blame her a bit," murmured the Big Business Man. "A man dropping from nowhere to carry her off—"

"Yes, sir," Loto agreed gravely. "But my intentions were the best, though she could not know it. Her attitude would be, perhaps, my greatest difficulty—and that is why I wanted my general appearance to be like the men of her own time.

"I left the plane. Besides the Collinger, I had a hand compass, and a small electric torch.

"It was very cold. I scrambled out through the snow, up the side of the gulley to the level land above—a climb of sixty or seventy feet.

"The snow was deep, with an underlying surface of snow or ice that would support my weight. Up here on the higher land it was colder than ever. The north wind hit me full; and I had been walking no more than five minutes when it began to snow."

Again Loto faced his mother. "You will say, *mamita,* that Providence was surely watching over me. I could not know it then, but if it had not snowed that night I should never have returned to you. But it did snow — tremendous flakes, that soon came in a thick, soft cloud, and blotted out everything around me.

"I had put into my pocket my fur cap with ear tabs. I soon found I would have to wear it, but I would take it off before there was any chance of the girl seeing me.

"I was heading across the wind, plowing through the loose snow. I could see only a few feet ahead of me. It was a pathless waste. And suddenly the whimsical thought came that I was crossing Fifty-Ninth Street, from the ferry, and soon I would be near Columbus Circle. It was the same space, the same location. Nothing was different but the time

—the changes time had brought." Loto smiled at his friends.

"The same space," murmured the Big Business Man. "Just think what an infinity of things that same space holds! Fifty-Ninth Street, from the ferry to Columbus Circle! Think of it in 1776! Or at the time of Christ! Or before the Stone Age!"

"And all the centuries between," the Doctor added.

"Or that gigantic city at its height, two thousand years from now," George put in. "Think of what that space held then!"

"I took out my compass," Loto resumed, "and by the light of my electric torch, I consulted it, heading as nearly as I could toward the house. So far as I had been able to tell before, there was no other habitation on the island.

"I suppose I struggled along for nearly an hour. I figured I must be in the vicinity of the house now —though I could see nothing but the snow covered ground a few feet ahead of me, the whirling flakes close at hand, and blackness overhead. Without warning, through a rift in the clouds to the east, came moonlight — a gigantic, egg-shaped moon with a reddish tinge to it that gave the scene a lurid, extremely weird look.

"The house was in sight, ahead and to the left on a slight rise of ground no more than a quarter of a mile away. I was faced now with the necessity for a definite course of action. From the laboratory, with my telescope, I had occasionally seen the girl late at night sitting in the central living room of the house. I had seen her through the transparent door and windows; and she had always left the public room to the southeast. The house faced south; I felt that her room was in the southeast end. The enclosure lay mostly behind the house — to the north, with the dog kennel in its extreme northern wall.

"This was all advantageous to me. I knew I had to keep down the wind from those dogs. With a wind of from twenty to thirty miles an hour blowing from them to me, I felt sure that they would not get my scent. My plan was to get into the house — either through a sort of gateway in the southeast wall of the enclosure or directly in through a window. I would locate the girl, carry her away —

by force, I suppose. I was confident — absurdly so, I realize now. I think it was the enthusiasm — the excitement of being actually engaged in what I had contemplated for two long years — had worked so hard to attain.

"My heart was beating fast as I crept forward, Collinger in my gloved hand. It was still snowing hard, and presently the clouds swept back over the newly risen moon; but I was now so close up that I could see the dark outlines of the house, and the wall of the enclosure.

"The building was only one story, but quite high, with a queer looking overhanging roof — mound shaped. The wall of the enclosure was some ten feet high. I circled to the south, and was soon close up to the main doorway of the house. The whole place was piled with snow. There was not a sound — only the wind howling as it swept in gusts under the low eaves.

"The glass door — I suppose it was glass — was a single rectangular pane in a dark narrow frame. It was no more than three feet broad, and at least twelve feet high. Behind it I could see the interior dimly lighted — a soft, blue-white light. I could not see where it came from.

"For quite a while I must have stood there motionless, peering in. A portion of a large room was in the line of my sight. It seemed unoccupied — a back wall hung with something dark; a sort of low couch to one side; queerly shaped, low chairs and a table or two. And there was a floor covering of some thick, soft textile, and several furs lying about — a large fur rug covering the couch.

"To the right I could see a low archway, hung with a curtain. That was in the direction of the girl's room. There were two other archways with curtains, but evidently no interior doors to the house.

"I had been pressing against the glass pane; it seemed to give a little. I pushed. The motion was inward, and greater at the bottom. I knelt down and shoved it. The lower half swung silently and smoothly inward and upward, while the upper half came out and down. The whole twelve foot pane was pivoted at its center. When it paralleled the floor it stopped, and there was a six foot opening for me to walk under and into the house.

"I took a cautious step, listening intently, peering around me — behind me — with the sudden feeling that something supernatural might leap forth — spring at me — any instant.

"But the Collinger in my hand — my finger on its trigger — gave me courage. In my left hand I held the electric flash light; and very slowly I crept toward the curtained archway behind which I hoped the girl might be. Suddenly I remembered my cap. I smiled at the absurdity of the detail — but nevertheless I pulled it off and stuffed it in my pocket. Then I went forward, pushed aside the curtain, and entered the space behind it.

"I was in darkness as the curtain dropped. It must have been a sort of anteroom, or a short hallway, for some twenty feet ahead of me I saw another curtain with a blue radiance beyond it.

"A moment more and I had pushed aside the further curtain and stood peering into the room beyond. It was more dimly lighted than the living room. Across it, in an angle of wall, the first thing my gaze caught was a low couch or divan, bathed in the blue radiance from a brazier beside it, which left the rest of the room in gloom. The girl lay there asleep. A soft, pure-white fur was covering her, but her bare arms and shoulders were above it. An arm was crooked under her head for a pillow — the other, white almost as the rug, lay stretched out over the fur. On her breast her golden hair lay in waves.

"I stood transfixed at the ethereal loveliness of the face, calm in deep slumber — a small oval face of seemingly perfect features, with soft, curving red lips slightly parted; smooth cheeks with a delicate rose color in them, and long dark lashes that lay motionless as she slept.

"My emotion at the picture was short lived — other thoughts crowded upon me. What was I to do? I could not awaken the girl and ask her to come with me. She would not understand the words, and if she did, she would probably have screamed before I could get them out. Seize her — stifle her cries and carry her off forcibly? That is what I should have done, perhaps — taken her to the plane and left explanations until afterward.

"But, gentlemen, you will understand me — I

could not bring myself to do that. Indeed, my whole instinct was to retreat from the room. I felt myself a gross intruder in a sanctified place, my very gaze an insult.

"What I should finally have done, I do not know. Events took the decision out of my hands. The wind outside roared with a sudden gust that must have pulled loose something under the eaves. There came a rattle, a thump, loud in the silence of the house. Then the wind died again.

"I glanced up to the ceiling, startled, with my heart pounding and the Collinger pointed toward the sound. I could see nothing but the dark rectangle of a window up there. My gaze fell again to the couch — and met the opened eyes of the girl! She was sitting up, her hair tumbling over her shoulders, one hand instinctively gripping the white fur to raise it more closely about her, the other pressed against her mouth. I think I could never imagine an expression of more utter terror than that on her face.

"I murmured something intended to be reassuring and made the mistake of taking a step forward. It was the worst thing I could have done, for her frightened scream rang out through the house.

"I tried to think quickly, but I realized now I was wholly confused. I turned back toward the curtain. I would escape from the house — come back some other time. Or should I pick her up now, and run with her? She was small — frail. I could carry her easily; escape almost as quickly with her, perhaps, as by myself. And shoot back at any one — anything — that followed.

"I found myself back at her couch. She had withdrawn to the further side of it, huddled against the wall. Her horrified eyes were on my face, but she did not scream again.

"There was a noise behind me. I swung about. The curtain was parting. There was a figure there. I could not see it plainly; it was in the darkness, and I was in the light. I aimed the Collinger, pressed the trigged. Simultaneously a tiny pencil-point of light seemed to spring at me from where the figure was standing — a brief, very tiny, but horrible intense glare flashed in my eyes.

"I was in darkness; everything went black. I did

not fall, but reeled sidewise. I heard a mocking laugh; footsteps running up to me; a hand struck me across the mouth.

"It is terrible to fight in total darkness. I stumbled aimlessly somewhere, and felt the Collinger twisted from me. But when I lurched in that direction, my outflung arms met only empty air. Again a hand struck me across the mouth; again that mocking laugh. My assailant was playing with me!

"I was unhurt, and desperately I rushed to where I thought the room's exit might be. But strong fingers gripped my shoulder and I was flung violently sidewise. I must have struck my head against something as I went down. My senses faded; the last thing I remember was that jeering, mocking laughter out of the darkness!"

CHAPTER VI.

ESCAPE.

"I CAME to myself still lying where I had fallen. Striking my head had knocked me out momentarily. I heard voices; some one was kneeling beside me.

"I opened my eyes, but everything was black. I remember feeling my head. It was not cut — only a lump on it. I was unhurt, and I struggled to a sitting position. Whoever it was beside me, now stood up and moved away. The girl's voice came to me out of the darkness. The low words were unintelligible — yet they were words not wholly unfamiliar in ring.

"The darkness was full of little darting red spots. And my eyes pained me — the backs of the eyeballs were burning. I was blind. I had not realized it —"

"Blind!" exclaimed George. "Oh, that little light he shot at you —"

"I had not realized it before, I thought the light

in the room had suddenly been extinguished — and a vague idea that my antagonist could see in the dark had possessed me. But it wasn't so. He had blinded me, with the tiny flash of light that had struck into my eyes.

"My head was still reeling from the blow when I fell. They carried me, half conscious, into some other room, and left me lying on something soft. I closed my eyes, but I could not shut out those darting red spots. At last, I must have drifted off to sleep.

"When I awoke it was morning. The red glow of the sunrise was coming in a small aperture up near the ceiling. I could see it; the blindness had passed. My head was still ringing, my eyes still pained me. But I was uninjured.

"I was on a low couch, with a fur rug under me. My overcoat lay beside me on the floor. The whole thing seemed like a dream to my mind, but finally I got it straightened out.

"I was in a fairly large bedroom. Two windows of heavy transparent material were up near the ceiling. Opposite to the windows was a doorway with a curtain. I slipped into my overcoat, searching its pockets. My cap was there, but the compass and the flashlight were gone and my Collinger had already been taken from me.

"The storm outside seemed to have passed. The house was dead silent. I went to the curtain; beyond it was a small hall, empty, and with another curtain at its further end. This I pushed aside cautiously. I was looking into the main living room of the house, and met the direct gaze of a man who was lounging there!

"I dropped the curtain hastily, but he had seen me and sprung to his feet — a powerful man, taller than myself, with gray, wide trousers and naked torso. I had retreated back to the bedroom — the fear of what he might do to me, blind me or worse, made me anything but anxious to encounter him again.

"He followed, and was upon me, twisting me by the shoulders to face him. He was a man of about thirty-five. Black hair, long to the base of his neck. Smooth-shaven — a strong, rugged face, with keen gray eyes beneath black, bushy brows; a nose a little like a hawk, and a wide mouth with thin lips. It was the sort of face that bespoke power — a nature born to dominate its fellows. And cruel, essentially cruel about the mouth. His gaze was searching — puzzled. I knew he was trying to make me out — wondering what manner of man I was — where I had come from. He spoke to me. I could not understand the words, but again I got the impression that they were familiar English words spoken differently. I answered; I don't remember what; but he frowned, and pushed me from him, toward the couch.

"I had decided to appear docile. I stumbled to the couch and sat down on it. He stood in the center of the room, regarding me; and I managed what I hoped might be an ingratiating smile. This seemed to appeal to him, for he smiled back. Then he swung about and left the room.

"For a while I sat quiet. The girl — where she was I did not know. I would have escaped without her if I could — but escape did not seem possible. At least, it was more of a risk than I cared to take. The feeling came to me that even now as I sat on the couch, I might be observed. How could I tell that some one was not watching me from behind some hidden orifice, through which, as I turned my gaze that way, that tiny, blinding beam of light would spring at me?

"It was too big a chance. I would wait, and when I knew better with what I had to contend, watch my opportunity to escape.

"The room was fairly light now — that queer reddish light. I could see the sky, brilliant with a glorious red sunrise, through the little windows overhead. I moved the table and climbed on it. Outside was snow, tinged with red. I was at an east end of the house, perhaps next to the girl's room.

"At a corner of the building nearby sat one of the dogs — like a gigantic shaggy wolf, quiet but alert. His head was fully six feet above the ground as he sat there squatting on his haunches. He heard me open the window, and trotted quietly over to look at me. My fascinated stare met his eyes squarely — eyes that seemed to hold an almost uncanny human intelligence. He seemed satisfied with the situation for he trotted back to the corner of the house, and sat down again. But he was still watching me.

"I dropped to the floor. The incident had left me shuddering. What manner of brutes were these, with gleaming tusk-like teeth, dripping jowls and a power in those tremendous muscles that must have far exceeded the strongest horse! And eyes that might have been human! I was further from thinking of escape that moment than ever.

"For three days they fed me in that room. A woman came mostly. She wore a loose, shapeless robe of dark cloth. It was dowdy-looking. Her hair was iron-gray, long, to her waist, twisted into a bundle and bound with strips of dark cloth. Her face was thin — careworn. She brought me my food — some kinds of cooked meats, and starchy vegetables, like potatoes. She was kind enough — but grim, as though I were an unpleasant task that her conscience made her discharge punctiliously.

"I tried to talk to her, but she couldn't understand me — nor I her. Afterward, I learned she was the older man's old maid daughter. The old man himself came in a few times — a smooth-shaven, stalwart man of seventy, perhaps, dressed in wide flowing trousers, and naked above the waist. Sometimes he wore a short little house jacket. His name was Bool. The younger man — the master of the house — was named Toroh. He came in and sat by me a few times, always intent to see that I was properly cared for. But there was no mistaking the fact that he would have killed me without compunction had I annoyed him; and I could not forget his sardonic laughter when he had blinded me."

"You fired the Collinger at him," George said suddenly. "Didn't you hit him? He wasn't — wasn't invulnerable to a bullet, was he?"

"No," Loto answered with a smile. "He was quite as human as I. He was standing in the shadow and I missed him. His blinding-flash struck my eyes just as I fired. I was telling you about my first three days in the house. I did not see the girl, except once, just for a moment. I was not held to the room, although I stayed there almost continuously. And one or the other of those dogs was outside all the time. After the first day, I grew bold enough to go into the living room.

"Once, when I was sitting alone in the main room, the girl entered. She stood in the doorway, and for the first time I realized how small and slight she was. She looked almost Egyptian—I mean her manner of dress. A blue-colored cloth was wound wide about her hips, with a dull red sash hanging knee-length down one side. Sandals on her bare feet; breast-plates of metal; a broad, low-cut collar of cloth with little coins on it, that lay flat on her upper chest and widened to cover her shoulders. And her golden hair was parted forward over her shoulders in plaits that ended with little tassels.

"Of course, I didn't see all those details then. She was standing there staring at me, and this time there was no fear in her eyes—only curiosity. My heart leaped; it was what I had hoped for most. I could do nothing toward planning to get her out of the house so long as she continued afraid of me.

"I smiled at her in as inoffensive and friendly a fashion as I could. Her eyes fell, then came up and I could see she was wondering at my clothes— my shoes, trousers, shirt and collar and tie. Abruptly the idea came to me that except for my garb, I probably did not look extraordinary or frightening to her. The thought gave me new courage. I stood up, and spoke. At once she turned and ran from the room.

"We were a strange household, but after a time, except for having my meals alone, I found I could move about pretty freely.

"Once Toroh brought me my electric torch, and, making sure I did not aim it at him, he made me light it. I knew he believed it a weapon. I thought this a good chance to convince him I was friendly. I smiled and shined it into my eyes, to show him it was harmless. He grunted and, taking the flashlight from me, tossed it across the room, as of no use or further interest.

"Then he produced my Collinger and made me show him how to operate it. But he was too clever to let me hold it; he did not let it get out of his hands. When he had fired it at a mark out the doorway, he grunted again and laid it on the snow. At a distance of twenty feet he stood with some object in his hand which he did not show me. Abruptly the Collinger flew into fragments! All its cartridges had been exploded simultaneously. The bullets whistled past us, startling Toroh as much as they did me. Later I learned he had exploded it by something akin to radio. He picked up the remains and when he got back into the house, he tossed my broken weapon away disdainfully. It was the attitude a soldier of to-day might have toward an Indian warrior and his bow and arrow."

"But what did these people think you were?" the Big Business Man demanded. "Some foreigner of their own world?"

"Toroh thought I had come from another planet. He had seen my plane the morning I hovered over the house. No one from another planet had been to the earth for centuries. But history told of them, and he thought I was one of them, come again. He treated me kindly enough — probably because I did not anger him or cross him in any way. But I had seen him strike the girl across the mouth; and one day he struck the woman. I have never seen such a look of sullen, repressed hatred as she gave him. She seemed to hate her father, too. Later, I often saw him cuff her when she annoyed him."

The Doctor would have interrupted, but Loto raised his hand. "I have so much to tell you. The girl—her name is Azeela. Toroh took two of his dogs and his sled and went away after about a week. He was gone a month. During that month I stayed docilely in the house. I saw many opportunities when I might have escaped. But now I would not, without taking Azeela, and I could not expose her to such danger as always seemed imminent.

"I must have convinced them all that I was harmless. No one paid me great attention except the woman—Koa. Often I would see her peering furtively at me from some distant doorway.

"Azeela soon became friendly, and since we both had nothing to do, she devoted herself to learning my language. I tried to learn hers and failed miserably. But she picked mine up with extraordinary rapidity. Perhaps because her mind was quicker— her memory more retentive. And I think also because she had behind her the inherited instincts of knowledge through all the centuries from my own time-world forward.

"At all events, within the month she could talk

my English freely enough for us to get along — with a quaint little accent wholly indescribable."

"*Your* English!" exclaimed the Doctor. "Was her language English also?"

"Yes, sir. I think it was derived very nearly from the English we speak to-day. Mine was, to her — merely archaic. But hers, modern beyond my time, was too much for me. It was an extraordinary story that Azeela had to tell me — as extraordinary as mine must have seemed to her. We became friends, and with her confidence came a renewed desire on both our parts to escape. Her people were many hundred miles away. And when I told her of my plane, I very soon persuaded her to let me take her back to her own country."

"Toroh hadn't found the plane?" George put in.

"No. If it had not snowed so heavily that first night, the dogs would have led him back over my trail to it. But it was still safe, though I did not know it then; and the thought that it might have been found bothered me a lot, I can tell you.

"We decided to try and escape. Toroh was ex-pected back any day. We spent a morning discuss-

111

ing it — planning it in detail. My weapons were gone — Azeela did not know where they were. Bool had a cylinder of the blinding-flash — I call it that because their name for it would mean nothing to you. But we could not get it; he kept it always about his person. The woman, Koa, we did not think was armed — though she might have been.

"Toroh had taken two of the dogs. There was one left, and almost continually it was pacing about the house outside. We realized that even if we succeeded in getting away with a few minutes' start, the dog would follow and overtake us before we could reach the plane.

"Bool was in one of the outbuildings nearly all that morning. Koa was moving about the house. We did not think she was listening to us; but she was, and evidently she had picked up something of my language — enough to give her the import of what we were discussing.

"She appeared suddenly, and with a furtive glance around, told Azeela she would help us escape. Azeela translated it to me, and the woman nodded grimly in confirmation. She was sorry for Azeela;

and she hated Toroh sufficiently to want the girl out of his clutches.

"Koa's plan was simple and it sounded eminently practical. She had no weapons, and did not know where any were, except those of her father, which she would not dare try to secure. But late that afternoon Bool would be in his room dozing. Koa would lock the dog in the kennel. Then we would be free to depart.

"The sun was almost setting that day when Koa informed us that the time had come. We had restrained our excitement; Bool had apparently not noticed anything unusual in our outward appearance during the day. He had retired to his room as customary, and Koa had taken the dog away.

"I did not altogether trust Koa, and it made me shudder to think of taking Azeela outside and perhaps have the dog spring upon us from somewhere. But we had to chance it, and the woman seemed sincere.

"We had searched the house as best we could without arousing Bool, but we found no weapon of any kind. At last we were ready, I in my fur coat,

113

Azeela in furs—shoes, trousers, and coat all one piece. She looked like a slender little Eskimo girl; and I smiled as she pulled up a fur hood that dangled at the back of her neck, and fitted it close about her face, tucking her hair up under it. I had been mistaken about headgear. It just so happened that I had never seen any one of this time-world except when they had been bareheaded.

"I put on my own cap and we were ready. As we met in the main room, Koa nodded sourly for us to be gone. At that instant the dog, outside in the kennel, gave a long mournful howl. I don't know why; I suppose it was just fate. Koa, waving us toward the doorway, hastened away to quiet the dog.

"For a moment I hesitated. Should we start? Had the dog got loose? That moment of hesitation was too long. Bool stood in the doorway, staring at our fur-covered figures. Astonishment, anger, rage swept over his face. His hand went to his belt; he jerked something loose. I heard Azeela give a sharp cry of warning. Bool's hand held an object like a little crescent of glass, with a tiny wire connecting its horns. Sparks darted from the wire.

"I was about to leap forward when suddenly I was stricken. I can only describe it as paralysis. I stood stock-still; my arms dropped inert at my sides. I felt no pain; but I was rooted to the spot, without power to lift my legs. Azeela, beside me, was evidently within the influence of the weapon also. She was standing rigid. Bool's face held a leer of triumph. His left hand was fumbling at his belt for some other weapon. I knew that in another moment he would have killed us. And still I could not move. I tell you, gentlemen, it was a ghastly feeling. There was a numbness creeping all over me. My hands were turning cold. My feet felt wooden. My legs were giving way under me, and in a few seconds more I think I should have fallen.

"It all happened very quickly. Behind Bool, Koa had appeared. He did not hear her; and she darted forward and struck at his wrist. The little crescent of glass dropped to the floor and was shattered. A wave of heat swept over me—the blood rushing again to my limbs.

"Bool had turned furiously upon Koa, but my strength was coming back fast. I jumped at them, caught Bool unprepared. My body struck his and we went down. He fell backward—I on top of him. His hand now held a metal cylinder; he was trying it get it up to my face.

"Azeela came darting across the room, threw herself upon us, and with her two hands twisted the weapon from Bool's fingers. I did not know she had done it. I was enraged. Bool was kicking, squirming, and his left hand had me by the forehead, pushing my head back to expose my face. I flung myself down on him, my forearm striking his head against the floor. His hold relaxed; he lay still.

"When I got to my feet, Koa was stooping over Bool. She seemed frightened at what she had done, although I knew well enough that the man had mistreated her constantly, and that she could bear him no great love. She waved us away—still with that same stolid grimness.

"'Ask her if the dog is fast, Azeela,' I said.

"The woman nodded at me vehemently, and I gripped Azeela's hand and we hurried out. It was just sunset. The sky was like blood; the snowy ground was all tinted with it.

116

"We ran west, so fast that Azeela could hardly keep her feet. It seemed ten miles, but it wasn't more than one or two. We slowed up and walked a little, then went back to a run. There was nothing but that unbroken expanse of snow, with the drop that was the river ahead of us.

"At last I could make out the break in the plateau surface that marked the gully. We were running, and were no more than fifty feet from it, when from behind us we heard the loud baying of the dog — that eager baying of a dog following a trail and close upon its quarry! I went cold all over. I knew what had happened. Bool had recovered, and in spite of his daughter had let loose the dog upon us!

"I caught a glimpse of Azeela's white, frightened face as I gripped her hand and jerked her forward. It was faster than carrying her. She stumbled, almost fell headlong, but I pulled her up and onward.

"We came upon the gully. For one agonized instant I wondered if the plane would still be there. The dog seemed almost upon us. I could hear its eager whine as it came leaping along. Then I saw the plane — snow-covered, but undisturbed.

"We flung ourselves down the gully side, sliding, falling to its bottom. The deep snow there broke our fall. The dog was at the top. I saw its huge head and its bared fangs as it dashed along, selecting a place to descend.

"I jumped to the cabin platform of the plane and shoved open the door. Then I stooped, grasping Azeela under the armpits and lifting her. The dog came sliding into the gully, and gathering itself up — it leaped.

"But we were inside, and I slid the door closed just as the brute's great body struck the cabin with an impact that rocked the plane. The dog fell, but was up again with a snarl, standing on its hind legs, its huge paws scratching at the cabin wall.

"I had flung Azeela to the floor of the compartment. She shouted at me reassuringly, and I jumped to the Frazia controls.

"A moment later the helicopters were raising us out of the gully. The dog's baffled yelps grew fainter. As we rose into the air I saw Bool, a quarter of the way from the house, stumbling along through the snow, following the trail.

118

"I went up a thousand feet, dropped a little, and began horizontal flight. To the south, perhaps a mile away, Toroh's sled, with its two dogs, was swinging up toward the house. He saw the plane, and as we swept over him at an altitude of some five hundred feet, he turned and followed us.

"It was amazing to see those two gigantic dogs run. They must have been pulling the sled at fifty or sixty miles an hour, for they kept almost under us. We came to the south of the island and they went down a declivity and out over the frozen, snow-covered water. Toroh was lashing them with a long quirt.

"I put on more power, and we gradually drew ahead. When we had crossed the broad expanse of bay, the sled was no more than a black blob in the distance. It swung to the right, turned and went back — lost to our sight in the gathering darkness.

"We were alone, fairly started southward to Azeela's native country and her people from whom Toroh had stolen her."

119

CHAPTER VII.

"I MUST GO THERE AGAIN."

For some minutes past the Big Business Man had been awaiting an opportunity to interrupt.

"I don't quite understand," he began, hestitantly. "I've been wondering — Loto, you spent a month in that house, but you've only been away from us some twenty-eight hours. We know. We've been right here. How could that be? You—"

"Your reasoning is quite wrong, Will," the Chemist exclaimed warmly. "Loto lived in that future time-world, went forward in it at its natural pace for the period of a month. Then he returned, back through time, and he stopped off at a point twenty-eight hours farther along than the point at which he started. Don't you grasp that?"

"I'd like to hear more about Azeela," George put in timidly. "Where was her home, Loto?"

Loto had refused George's proffered cigarette, and was fumbling in his pocket. He produced a little black pipe and lighted it before he went on.

"Azeela and her people live on an island which once was the mainland—the southeastern corner of the United States, as we know it to-day. It's a narrow, crescent-shaped island—something like Cuba in outline, but smaller. It is separated from the mainland by a channel some ten miles at its greatest width. It was for this island we were heading—south over what seemed almost a snow-covered waste. It was growing dark, but presently the moon rose—a red moon."

"And that red, burned out sun," mused the Big Business Man.

"No, sir. That's where you're wrong—totally wrong. The sun is not burning out. That sun was quite as hot, intrinsically, as the one that shone on you this afternoon. The red color is entirely atmospheric—a condition local to earth. It turned almost to yellow each day as the sun rose higher."

"But the cold—the snow and ice," protested the Doctor.

"Climatic conditions, apart from the sun," Loto answered.

"Climate is the most potent factor of all that influ-

121

ence mankind. This change throughout ten thousand years was dramatic in its effects. It hastened decadence. It drove civilization toward the equator. And then, as though nature were bent upon destruction, disease sprang up in the only warm regions left — disease that could not be coped with. Insects, carrying and transmitting deadly bacteria, swarmed over what we call the torrid zone, making it almost uninhabitable. An exodus from the earth began. The other planets took back their own — and millions of our people went with them.

"You must realize over how long a period this went on. The lifetime of an individual was only a tiny fraction of it. But at last the earth was again cut off. No one bothered to come here from other worlds. They had gone and left us — rats leaving a sinking ship.

"Even that was thousands of years before Azeela's birth. This island had formed, and nature had seemed to hold it the one place where humanity could make its last stand. A volcano stood at each end — beneficent, treasured because they contained heat. The internal fires of the earth had broken through here. Hot springs and geysers dotted the land. A river just below the boiling point rose from subterranean depths, flowed for a hundred miles, and plunged down again. And a huge range of mountains east and west on the mainland to the north offered shelter from the cold winds that were coming down.

"Upon this palm-covered, tropical island Anglo-Saxons with a strain of Latin settled long before the conditions farther north had become so drastic. They kept to themselves — fought against the pollution of their blood by others. They were of the stock of highest type of earth civilization — become decadent.

"For centuries they were left to themselves — to drift along in their own fashion. But with the coming of the cold the mixed races of the north began moving down — coveting the island. Then these island people suddenly sprang into activity. Defense of the homeland brought action. Lost arts of war were revived. The Anglese — that is as near the sound of their word for themselves as I can get — repulsed all comers.

"To the north was now a climate that held snow

123

from September to June. Only three brief months availed for agriculture. The mixed peoples there did not rise to master such rigors. Centuries of struggle turned them almost primitive — with arts and sciences and ways to conquer their environment lost and forgotten. They were barbarians.

"Such was the condition as I found it, gentlemen. I can give you details only of our northern half of the western hemisphere. Transportation was back nearly to the primitive; the rest of the world was almost unknown to Azeela's race.

"We flew the plane all that night, following the coast line south, over snow and ice, with villages here and there —"

Loto stopped abruptly; his gaze went to the windows of the small room in which they were sitting. The stars were growing dim in a brightening sky.

"Why, it's morning," he added. "I've talked to you all night. See, there!"

"All night," murmured the Big Business Man. "One night! And I feel as though I had lived millions of them!"

The Banker returned his watch to his pocket.

"Go on, boy. Did you get Azeela back to this island?"

"Yes, sir. And I found there a vital crisis impending. I— Oh, *mamita,* don't be worried! I must go there again."

Loto had turned impulsively to his mother. Lylda's breath was sharply indrawn, but she smiled.

"Go again?" Her low, anxious words were almost inaudible. Her fingers clung to his desperately. "Go again!"

"Yes, *mamita.* I can help them there. I even think they need me. And I—I want Azeela. I want to marry her."

His words were tumbling over one another. "Toroh was an Anglese, but they banished him. He was plotting to overthrow the government. When he was banished, he went among the barbarians of the north and began organizing them for an attack on the island. Toroh has scientific knowledge; up there in the north he has been manufacturing weapons. Then he came back to the island secretly, and abducted Azeela. She's the daughter of Fahn — leading scientist of the Anglese — the man who holds the reins of power. With Azeela as hostage, Toroh planned to make Fahn yield.

"But now I have released Azeela; and Toroh's attack will come swiftly. That is why I must return —I can help. Toroh is a menace—the greatest figure for evil of that time-world. There will be war—a struggle in which the Anglese may go down before the onslaught of Toroh and the hordes of barbarians with whom he has allied himself. Oh, I can't tell you all the details—I'm too tired."

Loto did look tired, as though all his reserve strength had suddenly left him. "I came back, because I was afraid I would run out of petrol for the plane. And the Proton current, too. And I wanted to tell you—about it all. You can follow me if I need you. I've thought of a way to convey to you that I want you to come." His pleading gesture was to Rogers. "Let me go there again, father. Please let me go there again!"

CHAPTER VIII.

THE SECOND DEPARTURE.

ONCE again, an evening later, the little company was gathered on the roof of the Scientific Club. The men had been examining the plane. Now they were standing in a corner of the board enclosure, bidding Loto good-by. Lylda seemed more composed at this second parting, but her eyes were misty as she kissed her son — to her still no more than a child.

"You've left directions for us, Loto?" she asked anxiously.

"Yes, *mamita*. With father. He will not open them until I have been gone a month. But, *'mita,* I will come back before then. You will see. It is nothing for you to worry over."

Beside the plane Loto shook hands gravely with Rogers.

"You have my letter, father? It explains everything fully. But do not open it until a month has passed."

"No," Rogers agreed.

"It might worry *mamita*," Loto added softly. "I will come back before a month, no doubt. And to worry her would be unnecessary."

The Banker and the others joined them.

"Boy," said the Banker, "there were a lot of things you didn't tell us last night."

"Yes, sir," Loto agreed smilingly. "But later I can tell you. I have had so much to do to-day—"

George's hand on his arm made him turn.

"I want to speak to you—alone," George said soberly. His face was flushed; he seemed laboring under tremendous excitement. "Alone—just a minute." Loto took him aside. "Listen," George added swiftly. "I'm an orphan, you know. I haven't got a soul in this world, I guess, who cares a rap about me. I've made all my plans to-day—been at it every minute." He stopped and drew a deep breath. "I'm going with you! Listen, please let me go! Nobody 'll miss me—nobody 'll care if I'm gone forever." A note of pathos was in his eager, pleading voice. "Please let me go—I can help you a lot. You don't realize it, maybe, but I can."

Loto recovered from his surprise, hesitated, then shook his head.

"Oh!" said George, crestfallen. "Why not? Don't you think I can help you?"

"Yes, but"—Loto bent closer to him—"George, here's the truth, just between you and me. Not a word to the rest?"

"No!" George was thrilled.

"Well, listen. I'm liable to get into things as dangerous as the devil. You don't know anything about it—I didn't want to tell them last night."

"All the more reason why you ought to have me with you," George declared.

"No. You see—well, I might never come back. And if I don't, if I'm not coming in ten years—twenty years—you'll know it a month from now. Father has a paper from me explaining all that."

"What of it? Why shouldn't I go along with you—"

"No. Father will want to follow me, and I'm counting on *you* to join him."

George was somewhat mollified. "Oh! Sure I'll do that."

"But not a word now?"

"No. But, say, Loto, don't bother to come back, will you? Give us a chance to come on after you."

Loto laughed. "All right. Maybe I won't come back. I'll count on you, anyway."

They shook hands solemnly.

"You bet," George agreed. "And give my regards to Azeela. You didn't say you mentioned me to her."

"I didn't. I was pretty busy. But I will, George."

"Right. Do that. Good luck, old man!"

Within five minutes more Loto was again in the plane, with its cabin door closed upon him. Again that queer, insistent humming. The plane glowed phosphorescent — seemingly brighter now, for the lights of the enclosure had been extinguished. Then that translucency of the solid cabin walls and the huge, spreading wings; a fleeting instant when they seemed vapory — a shimmering mist dissolving into nothingness. Then only the memory that the plane had been there, but now was gone.

CHAPTER IX.

THE MESSAGE.

An evening in September. Loto had been gone a month. Almost constantly some one of his four friends, or his father or mother, had been about the rooftop. But the Frazia plane had not appeared; the board enclosure where it had rested was empty.

The fear in Lylda's eyes had grown daily almost into terror. But she had not spoken of it, and her husband's consoling, hopeful words — couched sometimes in the seemingly cold, logical phrases of science — she had received with a brave, pathetic smile.

The month of waiting — almost interminable to them all — had passed; and now, at Rogers' request, they were again secluded in a private room of the club. Rogers sat by the center table, in the circle of illumination of the electrolier, with a sheaf of penciled script in his hand, and a torn envelope beside him. The men were facing him, expectant. Lylda sat in the shadows near by, staring before her into vacancy.

"A month," Rogers was saying. "It has seemed longer. I opened Loto's letter this afternoon — and then I telephoned to you all. Let me read you the message he left us."

He adjusted his horn rimmed spectacles. The men stirred in their chairs; George lighted a cigarette and began puffing at it vigorously.

"It says:

My Father and my Friends:

When you read this I shall have been gone from your time world for thirty of its days. You will know that I am not coming back. Had I been forced to stay ten or twenty years of time as I would have lived them, I would still return to the exact evening — or before it — on which you are reading this letter.

That was my promise to you, father. The fact that I am not returned will let you know that probably I am never coming.

Mamita must not worry, for I gave you another promise. When danger threatened me — or when I wanted your help — I would raise a light signal so that you, coming after me, might know exactly what point of time at which to stop your flight.

As I write this, now before leaving you, I renew that promise. When I find I cannot return, I will raise a light from the southeastern tip of the island. I will hold it in the sky for a day and a night. You will see it, if your time flight is slow enough, and I shall know that when I extinguish it you will be there.

Tell *mamita* I shall not wait for danger, but anticipate it. You will see my light, no matter when I raise it. A year after I get there — or ten years — it will be no different to you who follow me — only a few minutes of time progress in your plane. I shall expect you as soon as you can descend after seeing the light vanish. Do not delay then, father, for I will need you.

Please tell *mamita* not to worry about me, or about you, either. We will both come back to her safely. You may bring any one or two of our friends who wish to make the trip. I think that George will want to come, and I would like to have him. You need bring no weapons. They would be worse than useless.

LOTO.

Rogers' slow, solemn voice died away. He rustled the pages in his hand, folded them up carefully.

"That's all, gentlemen. All of the message itself. The other pages give detailed instructions — data based on Loto's first flight and memoranda for the construction of another plane, gathered from previous notes made by Loto and myself."

There was complete silence when Rogers paused. George decided to speak, but checked himself and relaxed back in his chair.

"I shall start the Frazia Company on another plane at once," Rogers added. "And working on Loto's mechanism simultaneously, I should be ready in ninety days."

He waited, but again no one else spoke. Then he said:

"I am going, of course. It is a great trial for my wife, but she is willing."

George turned and flashed an admiring glance to Lylda; her face was strained, but she smiled at him gently.

"Do not be hasty, my friends," Rogers went on quickly. "Any two of you are free to come — or to stay, all of you — as you think best."

"I'm going," said George suddenly. "Loto said I could. And you say so. I'm going. I decided that long ago."

He jumped to his feet and grasped Rogers' hand. "You can count on me, Mr. Rogers. I'll stick — through anything — to the last."

Rogers smiled. "Thank you, George. I knew I could count on you."

George sat down again. Then he got up and

crossed to Lylda, shaking her hand also, and whispering to her. But in another instant he was pacing the room, smoking violently, and frowning.

Rogers was saying to the others: "I will take one more. I realize it is a momentous question. Your lives may be at stake."

The Big Business Man was deep in reverie. "I wonder," he murmured. "I wonder if I *do* want to go! I've known right along I'd have to make this decision."

"Come on," urged George, stopping suddenly before him. "Take a chance." He did not wait for an answer, but went back to his pacing.

"I don't think *I'll* go," the Banker declared, half apologetically. "You don't really need me, do you, Rogers?"

"Of course not," said Rogers heartily. "Use your own judgment. But I knew you'd be offended if I didn't give you the opportunity."

The Banker nodded. "Yes, but you don't need me. I'm an old man — seventy-three, though you'd never guess it, perhaps. I think I'd better stay where I'm used to things."

"Of course," agreed Rogers.

"But if you need money," the Banker added hope-fully, "you will, naturally — everybody needs money — you'll call on me, won't you? I'm going to see this thing through."

"I don't believe I'll go," the Big Business Man declared. He met the Doctor's glance, and the Doctor seemed relieved. "You don't really need us, Rogers? I think Frank would prefer to stay also."

The Doctor nodded emphatic agreement.

"Quite so," said Rogers. "I can understand per-fectly how you feel."

George stopped his pacing. "Then it's all settled, Mr. Rogers. You and I go — the others stay on guard here. Now listen, everybody, I've got some good ideas —"

CHAPTER X.

THE FLIGHT THROUGH TIME.

Two days before Christmas. Another plane lay glistening on the roof of the Scientific Club, walled in from curious eyes by the board enclosure. Sleek, self-satisfied, its every line denoting latent power, it lay motionless, awaiting those human masters who soon were to launch it into another time world.

Occasionally during the afternoon it was visited anxiously by a slim, boyish figure — George, who was verifying again and again that all was in readiness.

Evening came. The others arrived, singly and in couples. For two hours a bustle of last preparations went on — things forgotten, last minute plans put into execution. But by nine o'clock the moment of departure was finally at hand.

The Banker was in a fluster of excitement. He had appointed himself the leader of those who were

137

to be left behind, and he felt the responsibility keenly.

"Tell me exactly what we've got to do," he insisted. "I don't want anything to go wrong."

Rogers slapped him on the back. "It's nothing to be alarmed over."

"No. But I want to be sure I've got it straight. Tell me all over again."

Rogers repressed a smile. "When we have gone you will all wait some ten minutes — to be sure nothing has gone wrong to bring us immediately back. Then you will lock up the enclosure and leave. I have made arrangements with the club to have the enclosure left standing."

"That's all?" asked the Banker anxiously. "We leave the roof open?"

"Yes. In coming back we will want it open — and you cannot tell when we may return."

"But no more than six months?" the Banker insisted. "You promise that?"

Rogers nodded.

"Come on," George's voice called. "Let's get started." He had shaken hands with Lylda and

138

climbed up to the doorway of the cabin. "Come on, Mr. Rogers. Let's get started."

Lylda stood apart. Her farewell to her husband was brief. The others turned away, feeling that they should not intrude upon it. When Rogers had joined George on the platform of the plane the Doctor was with Lylda comforting her.

With a final good-by Rogers slid the door closed. The forward compartment, with its low arch ceiling and its concave walls, was small, but comfortably equipped. The side windows had upholstered seats running under them. In front, to the right, was a low seat with the Frazia controls before it, and a small window above them looking forward. The time dials and the Proton current switch were on the wall to the right. On the left of this seat was the outer, sliding door.

The division wall between the forward compartment and the engine room behind it held a small doorway with a sliding door.

"Are we ready?" Rogers asked. "I think we should be sitting. The shock of departure — new to us — may be more severe than we anticipate."

His words were calm enough, but they sent a thrill of excitement through George. "All ready," he said. "Go ahead!"

Rogers took a last look about. Then without hesitation, he moved the switch to the first intensity.

George was seated, gripping the arms of his chair. The humming seemed very different now than when he had heard it outside the plane. It was no louder, but it seemed to hum and vibrate inside his body. He was quivering inside; his head began reeling dizzily; there came that sickening, horrible sensation of falling headlong — a vertigo that turned everything to blackness.

"Are you all right? We've started."

It was Rogers's anxious voice, George opened his eyes; everything seemed glowing, unreal, and ghostlike. But he was uninjured; and his head had steadied.

"I'm all right," he managed to say.

The sickness passed quickly. George stood up, steadying himself. "Gosh, how light I feel! Queer in the head — don't you? I never imagined —"

He stopped abruptly. Through a side window

the fur-coated figure of the Banker was standing against the wall with the others around him. They were staring at the plane with an expression that clearly indicated they could not see it.

"We've started all right," George added. "Look at them! We're already in future time to them. They can't see us!"

Suddenly the Banker came forward walking with extraordinary swiftness, and seemingly with little jerks, like a manikin. George held his breath, for the Banker popped forward, his head and shoulders piercing the glowing phosphorescent walls and floor of the cabin. He stood motionless a brief instant, his face close to George's knees. Then, even more rapidly than he had advanced, he threw a swift glance around and retreated.

George recovered himself. "Oh," he said. "Wasn't that weird though? But we're all right. I feel fine now."

The droning of the Frazia motors sounded very faintly above the humming. It was a relief — a help toward normality. The plane was slowly raising into the air.

As it mounted, the roof of the Scientific Club dwindled away below. It was a dark night, with heavy clouds, and a cold wind from the east. The city, with snow on its rooftops, was sliding eastward beneath them — vague black shadows, dark buildings dotted with lights, and seemingly empty streets.

They were still mounting diagonally upward, drawn vertically by the helicopters and carried sidewise by the wind, when the Hudson River slid underneath.

"Rotten weather, Mr. Rogers," George suggested.

"Yes," Rogers agreed. "But that will not bother us for very long. Are you warm enough?"

"One heater is going," George responded. "I'll switch on another." He had familiarized himself throughly with the various mechanical appliances of the plane, and he turned a switch that threw current into another of the small electric radiators.

"Anything else?" he demanded.

"No, I think I shall try the higher intensities of the Proton current. I want our time-progress accelerating as much as possible right from the beginning."

142

George selected a seat hastily.

It was not much of an ordeal. The humming seemed to move up a scale, to a higher pitch as Rogers pulled the lever around. The reeling of the senses came again, but passed almost at once.

"There," said Rogers' voice. "I'm glad that's accomplished. We are at the fifteenth intensity — the highest that Loto used."

George was staring down through the floor window. "I can see lights down here. The highest speed Loto used? Why he didn't describe it this way —"

"Our acceleration will pick up over several hours," Rogers replied. "Our time-progress is still comparatively slow."

The drone of the Frazia motors was still sounding.

"How high are we, do you suppose?" George demanded after a moment.

"Possibly five thousand feet. We're blowing westward over New Jersey. And a little to the south, I think. Soon it will be —"

His words were anticipated. The scene lighted swiftly. It was day — a dull, cold-looking, cloudy

143

morning. Below them lay New Jersey—almost a network of villages on the fringe of lowlands. A more congested area of buildings was almost directly beneath and slid under them as they watched it.

"Newark!" exclaimed George. "And we're into to-morrow. We're making it—we'll soon be with Loto."

They were up higher than Rogers realized—ten thousand feet, at least. And their drift seemed constantly of a more southern trend. It was still uncomfortably cold in the cabin.

"Perhaps we should stay at this level," Rogers remarked. "We seem to have caught a wind from the north."

He slowed down the helicopters until the plane was no longer rising. As though they had been in a balloon, they were hanging level, blowing over the country—nearly south at some twenty miles an hour.

Night came again in a few moments. Lights dotted the landscape below—but they were vague, flickering lights. Then day, with sunlight. The wind subsided. The plane's southern drift was stilled. And then came night with a moon plunging across the sky, and stars dizzily sweeping past. Then day again, until presently the daylight and the darkness were blended into gray. The drift was permanently passed. In a blending of all the diversified air currents, the plane remained almost stationary.

The white, snowy hills of New Jersey soon turned to green. The cabin air warmed a little. Then autumn and winter came again — and passed in a moment or two.

Rogers sighed with relief. "We're fairly started. One year out of twenty-eight thousand!"

"And we've got eight hundred or a thousand miles of space to travel also," said George. "We're going to make that simultaneously, aren't we?"

"Yes," agreed Rogers.

George took a last look through the floor window at the blurring gray landscape beneath, and stood up to join him. "Let's talk things over," he suggested. "I've got a lot of questions — plans and things."

Rogers had taken a sheaf of script from his pocket. "Loto's notes to guide us," he explained. "I've

145

followed them closely so far. We have a flight through time of something more than twenty-five thousand years at the fifteenth intensity, and then slacken. Simultaneously we must fly southward, some thousand miles or more through space, directing our course for the southern tip of Florida. Loto specifies that we should under all circumstances reach the latitude of north Florida coincident with twenty-five thousand years of our time-progress. We will then — or perhaps a thousand years further along — see the island. We cannot miss it, of course. It is so large, and it must certainly endure over a great period of time."

"How long did Loto take to reach twenty-five thousand years?"

"About twelve hours," Rogers consulted the memoranda. "He computes his average speed as equivalent to the twelfth intensity. We are using the fifteenth continuously. Our clocks should register no more than ten hours for the time-flight.

"Ten hours," he added thoughtfully. "And flying directly south at a hundred miles an hour we would reach the island in those ten hours."

146

"But we haven't started flying yet," George protested. "We're moving through time all right, but we're still right over Newark — and look at it!"

The New Jersey metropolis was spreading west to the Orange Mountains, and eastward, already it seemed linked solid with Jersey City. Factories dotted the intervening meadows, which now were drained of their stagnant water.

"You're right," exclaimed Rogers. "We have barely nine hours left — we must start our horizontal flight."

In a few moments more they were speeding south, and slightly west, at an altitude of some five thousand feet, with their progress through time steadily accelerating.

An hour, by their clocks, had passed. They were over Delaware Bay. Its shores seemed in the more congested areas almost solid with buildings. There was a great city on each side at the mouth of the river, with a gigantic bridge connecting them. The bridge rose into being under the eyes of the watchers in the flying plane, but they swept on past and in a moment left it far in the distance behind them.

George was seated on the floor watching the changing landscape — a huge, concave gray surface, shadowless, stretching out and up to the circular horizon. Steadily, like a panorama unrolled, it slid sidewise beneath them. The motion was greatest directly below. To the west the mountains seemed, by an optical illusion, to be following, speeding forward with them.

The sea or its arms constantly occupied a portion of the scene, for they were still flying south and somewhat west, following the Atlantic coast. And of everything in sight, the sea only seemed unchanging.

In time-progressing, that height of civilization Loto had described lay under them. They were flying lower now.

Rogers in his seat at the controls said: "I think we're making it as we should. That's the four thousand year mark just passed. And we are flying at a hundred and ten miles an hour."

"Are you sure we'll hit it right?" George asked anxiously.

"I think so. It is about as Loto figured so far.

148

Those buildings — what a civilization that must be down there. It will fade presently. In three or four thousand years —"

George joined him at the forward window. "Where are we? Are we still over Virginia?"

"Yes, at least I think we haven't crossed into North Carolina yet. That was Chesapeake Bay a while ago. Look! That city there! It's melting — going down fast! What changes time does make! How little of it we can see or realize in a lifetime!"

The cabin interior was unlighted and dark, save for that phosphorescence with which everything glowed. In their absorption in the scene below, the travelers had forgotten their own curious aspect, until George suddenly remarked:

"Look at us! Ghosts flying through space! Doesn't it make you feel queer, Mr. Rogers?"

The dim cabin interior, with its vague, luminous human figures, did indeed seem unreal. But the unreality was matched now by the scene beneath; their forward flight through space, combined with a time-progress now tremendously accelerated, made everything below a shifting, sliding kaleidoscope of changing effects that the eye could see, but the mind grasp only imperfectly. Details were transient things blurred one into the other.

The broad fundamentals, however, were obvious. The gray, concave land, ridged with mountains, the indented coast line, the gray, changeless sea — all were distinguishable. And overhead spread the sky, blurred and gray also — luminous with the mingled light of sun and moon, and a myriad starry worlds, and blended darker by nights of rain and snow and storm.

CHAPTER XI.

THE LIGHT ON THE ISLAND.

They were over North Carolina when Rogers, at the Frazia controls, grew tired. The clock stood at two five. They had been gone some five hours.

"I must rest," said Rogers. "George, can you take my place?"

George hesitated. "I've flown a bit. But never in a Frazia. I think I'd better not experiment—not on this flight."

"All right," Rogers agreed. "I'll use the helicopters for a while. Half an hour will rest me up."

In a few moments they were hovering, seemingly motionless, over North Carolina. Far away to the east, over a bulge in the coast line, they could just make out Cape Hatteras, with the ocean beyond it.

Rogers stretched himself out on one of the leather seats, and lighted a cigar. George sat beside him.

"I figure we should be at least halfway to the

northern coast of the island," the older man said. "We have flown some four hundred miles in four hours."

"But Loto will be waiting at the southeastern tip of the island," protested George. "That will be easily two or three hundred miles further, won't it? I wonder how far along we are in time."

"Look at the dials."

George bent over them. "Sixty-five hundred years. About that. Some of the hands are going too fast to read."

"More than I had thought," commented Rogers. "Do you figure we're still accelerating?"

"I think we have just about reached our greatest speed," Rogers answered slowly. "Let us see. We've done an average of thirteen hundred years an hour. We must be progressing at double that now."

George was figuring on the back of an old envelope. "Twenty-six hundred an hour. In five more hours at that rate we'll be close to twenty thousand. We can fly down to the north coast of the island easily by then."

"Exactly. We are a little ahead in our space

flight. I'm glad of it. We shall have to slow our time-progress to almost nothing at the end. We must take no chances of missing Loto's light signal."

"Twenty-six hundred years an hour," mused George. "That's what we're making now. Forty-five years a minute. A century almost every two minutes!"

The clock had registered thirty minutes more when Rogers declared he was sufficiently rested. At George's suggestion they had eaten a light meal; then again they started their flight southward.

"How about looking at the dials again," George remarked. "They were at sixty-five hundred, thirty minutes ago."

"Eight thousand," Rogers read. "That's fifteen hundred more. It figures three thousand an hour. That is our peak, I think."

The flight now was under constant conditions — in every two minutes the plane was passing some three or four miles of space and a century of time. They crossed above North Carolina, and came to the coast again. The cities of the civilization beneath them seemed breaking up. Here and there one

153

stood in its glory; others were mere deserted piles of ruins over which the vegetation was crawling with an eagerness to devour. Still other cities and villages appeared over the southern horizon, sturdy and whole — and melted as they slid beneath the plane into crumbling piles that passed out of sight to the north.

Soon desolate areas appeared. The scene grew vaguely whiter; the snow was coming down from the north faster than the plane was flying. Changes in the coast line became apparent; unfamiliar arms of the sea swept into view, and were crossed and left behind. A small, unfamiliar island lay close to the South Carolina coast. But as a whole, the land and sea held their own — even against the ravages of so many centuries.

"We're making more than a hundred miles an hour," Rogers said suddenly. "A hundred and twenty-five at least. The north wind is with us — the wind Loto described that blew southward almost all the year. What time is it?"

"By the clock or the dials?"

"The clock. I have the dials here. Eighteen

thousand four hundred years is their reading."

"Quarter of six," announced George.

"We should sight the island shortly," Rogers said. "I'll fly a trifle slower. We must be nearly down to the State of Georgia by now—to where Georgia used to be, I should say. I want to sight the island at twenty thousand years, or thereabouts."

Rogers was very tired—as much from trying to grasp the gigantic changes flowing beneath him, as from flying the plane.

The land was growing white; the vegetation sparser. Small towns and hamlets that endured for no more than fifty or a hundred years—shadowy, vague and unreal with their changing form—now were springing up everywhere and melting into nothing in a moment or two. The vegetation was shifting—changing. But always the scene was growing whiter. The villages were sparser, smaller and shorter lived—a people struggling southward against the threatening, irresistible cold, which spared nothing but the island of the Anglese.

The cataclysm which formed this island may have come at ten thousand years—beyond our present—

or at twenty. At all events, the island was there when the plane reached its space and its time. Rogers was first to notice a radical departure from the normal conformation of the landscape. They were, by their own calculation, over Georgia; George, watching the dials closely, had just noted twenty-two thousand years. Far ahead, over the rim of the southwestern horizon, a line of mountains was rising.

"Look!" exclaimed Rogers softly. "The mountain chain running east and west! The new mountains! The island must be just beyond them."

He drove the plane into a climb—a long incline up to higher altitudes. The gray land and sea tilted and began dropping away. The mountains seemed following up—higher and closer; until at last the plane was over them, barely a thousand feet above their rocky spires.

It was a scene of wild grandeur that now spread out beneath the eyes of the watchers in the plane. Crags were tumbled about; dark, riven cliff faces, with snow capped summits. A peak pure white; a gray blue valley beside it. And the whole as a mass was reared ten thousand feet above the sea.

The plane swept forward; the jagged, tumbled land slid northward close beneath it. Then, abruptly, the crags and peaks dropped away. It was as though the plane had leaped ten thousand feet into the air. Far below lay a narrow channel — gray water stretching east and west. And beyond that another land, its outer coast curving to the south.

"The island!" exclaimed Rogers softly. "What a cataclysm was here — a rift that let the sea in, and buckled up the mountains!"

Looking behind them, the travelers could see the southern slopes of the range, with a greenish verdure shifting and crawling — verdure that was green, but with a whitish cast, for in the winters the snow was coming down from the peaks above.

"The island!" echoed George. "And we're at twenty-three thousand five hundred years! We've some distance yet to fly," he warned. "Hadn't we better slacken our time progress?"

With their flight through space temporarily checked, the helicopters holding them motionless, Rogers cut down the Proton current to the fifth intensity. Eagerly they looked below them.

Beyond the channel lay the island, curving up in an arc from the south and out to the west. They could not see across it, but only to a ridge of mountains at its center. Huge palms lay thick upon it everywhere; a broad, curving beach of white sand edged it. An island Paradise — though their time progress still laid a gray cast over the green, blurred the water into a formless haze along the beach and shifted the vegetation into a confusion of changing forms.

"We must get started," said Rogers at last. "At twenty-eight thousand years we must be within sight of the southern tip."

It was a flight almost due South. Lakes occasionally were visible, two or three small rivers, one of which changed its course suddenly under their eyes; and everywhere that same tropical verdure, mounting and melting — always shifting with its rapid growth and decay.

In some three hours more, with another longer rest for Rogers during which helicopters held them poised motionless — they sighted the southern tip of the island. It had narrowed here to a point no more than two miles wide, ending with a curving beach and the broad, empty ocean beyond — a beach with a palm covered mountain slope close behind it.

Rogers had made several changes of time progress during the latter part of the trip; and they were poised over the sea near the tip of the island no more than a few moments when the dials recorded twenty-eight thousand two hundred years.

Rogers consulted Loto's notes. "He landed in this time world at twenty-eight thousand two hundred and four years. We must stop at the beginning of that year, and watch for his light."

Using the fourth intensity, the daylight and darkness was separated into two brief, but distinguishable periods. Thus the voyagers sped through the days and nights, the months and forward into another year. At the beginning of the fourth year of that new century, Rogers changed to the third intensity. It was daylight — a yellow-red, swiftly mounting sun, with flying blurs of white clouds close overhead; a blue sea, and a bright green island at the side.

The sun plunged across the sky and sank blood-red, with an instant of glorious colors suffusing the western sky. Night came, with its deep, purple mystery. Then day again.

Thus the days of that fourth year went by—each hardly a minute long, but slow to the two men so anxiously watching. They were tired to the point of exhaustion; but the excitement and anxiety kept them up.

"He said from the tip of the island," Rogers murmured. "A blue-white, vertical beam of light into the sky. For a day and a night. We couldn't miss it. A minute would show it to us plainly."

"I haven't taken my eyes off that island for a second," commented George from his seat on the floor. "Why doesn't he hurry up? He got here in January or February. It must be June or so already. He's down there, why doesn't he give us the signal?"

Rogers did not answer. The sun dropped below the horizon. The turning world, with its motion made so visible, was dizzying to one who watched the sky.

The purple night was colored with a moon—red as it rose and swiftly plunged into a thick bank of clouds that swept down upon it.

Abruptly, from the tip of the island a shaft of blue-white light shot into the sky. It wavered an instant; then stood motionless — clear, distinct, unmistakable!

CHAPTER XII.

THE HOUSE IN THE JUNGLE.

THE Proton current had been entirely cut off. The interior of the cabin was solid in appearance once more. The Frazia helicopters were still droning; the plane hung motionless in a night that was without wind. Below it now lay a scene of complete normality. The sea was rolling up on the white sand. The green island was bathed in moonlight — a moon almost at the zenith now — a small moon, silver, tinged with red, with a red-white, fleecy cloud slowly floating nearby. And from the tip of the island, quite near its southern branch, Loto's narrow beam of blue-white light was flashing upward into the sky.

They descended, not with the helicopters, but in a gentle glide. The beach was broad and firm. They landed upon it, swooping along. It was like racing an automobile along the sand in the moonlight, with the ocean on one side — far out at low tide now; and on the other side a jungle of green tropical vegetation.

Rogers, at the controls, saw a number of human figures standing on the beach ahead of him. They scattered hastily, and the plane, rapidly losing velocity, went past them and stopped a hundred yards farther.

"We're here!" cried George. "Let's get out. Was that Loto we passed? Where's the light? Are we near it?"

The light could be seen no more than a hundred feet away among the palms. They climbed hastily from the plane. A figure was coming forward along the beach at a run — a slight figure in wide trousers of white cloth, a short, flapping jacket, and bareheaded.

"Loto!" shouted George. "That you, Loto?"

The figure answered: "Hello-o — George!" It increased its speed. It was Loto.

"Oh," he exclaimed, as he shook their hands. "You got here right away, didn't you? I've only had that light up two or three hours."

"We're tired out," said Rogers, when the greetings

163

were over. "Do we stay in the plane, or can we leave it?"

A man was standing fearfully at the edge of the green jungle nearby. Loto called him forward—a man in wide trousers, like Loto's, except that they were smeared with dirt and sand; and with bare feet and naked torso. He came, timidly, and Loto spoke to him apart. The man nodded his head, with understanding of his orders. Then he trotted away, joining three or four others of his kind, gesticulating toward the plane. After which they all approached it reluctantly.

George plucked at the flaring sleeve of Loto's short jacket—his only garment above the waist. "How's Azeela, Loto? Is she—is everything all right?"

"Yes. She's all right. But—I thought I needed you and father here. Wait! Not now. I'll tell you later."

Rogers joined them. "We're about exhausted, Loto. We must have some sleep."

"Yes, sir. I knew you'd be. I've a house near here —only a hundred yards or so. They'll guard the plane." His gesture indicated the men who were now on the sand, moving about the plane, but evidently afraid to touch it.

"You can trust them?"

"Yes, sir. Implicitly."

They followed Loto. George was tired, but so excited that he did not realize it. The night air was warm and heavy with moisture. It was oppressive, it reminded him somehow of the steam room of a Turkish bath. He found himself perspiring.

They left the moonlit beach, and following a tiny white-sand path, plunged into the depths of the jungle. Palms of every variety stood about, their graceful fronds interlacing overhead. There were huge banana trees, loaded with fruit, mangoes, grapefruit — other fruit trees that George dimly remembered having heard of but could not name; and others that he was sure were entirely new.

It was dark in the jungle here, and very silent. The steamy air was redolent with perfume — orange blossoms, George told himself. The light-signal was nowhere to be seen. George wondered if it had burned out, or if Loto had ordered those men to extinguish it.

165

"Here we are," said Loto abruptly.

A house was standing at the right, in an open space with the moonlight gleaming on it — a large, tropical-looking bungalow. There was a broad veranda on three sides, with windows opening into the house. The whole was raised some four feet off the ground on coconut posts; and a brown thatched roof spread over everything like a mound.

It seemed a house that might have ten rooms at least. George wondered what made it look so peculiar. Then he realized that its board walls were not vertical, but sloped inward toward the top, so that its rooms would be smaller at the ceiling than the floor. It looked like a house of cards.

Loto had turned into another path. A brown picket fence enclosed the house with perhaps an acre of ground. Inside was a flower garden through which they passed. There bloomed beside them an extraordinary profusion of flowers; which, with the warm, moist air, made George feel he was in a hot house at some horticultural exhibit.

A short flight of wooden steps led to the veranda. There Loto stopped.

"I think we should retire at once," said Rogers. "We have so much to talk of — but it will wait, Loto?"

"Yes," Loto agreed. "Come with me, father. George, you stay here. I'll be right out."

George sat down on the veranda, with his back against a round palm-trunk that was supporting its roof. He realized now how tired he was — and this heavy air made him sleepy. He heard the others moving away — entering the house. He took off his coat — then his shirt; and using them rolled for a pillow stretched himself out at full length on the board flooring of the veranda.

In a moment, when Loto returned to take him to the room they were to occupy together, he found George sleeping peacefully.

CHAPTER XIII.

A MESSENGER FROM THE NORTH.

GEORGE awakened with the morning sun streaming through a window. He was on a broad couch, and in a chair beside him, Loto was reclining comfortably, smoking his little black brier pipe. He smiled.

"Oh, you're awake, are you? You ought to be — it's hours after sunrise."

A vague memory of being taken into the house by Loto the night before came to George. He remembered being half-asleep and talking to his friend; but it was all like a dream.

The room was small — queer-looking with its walls sloping together toward the ceiling. But it was bright and clean, with fibre brown matting on the floor.

The air was as moist and heavy as ever — and even warmer. George sat up, mopping his forehead with his shirt sleeve.

"I've got your clothes," said Loto. He indicated a stool with garments lying on it. "You don't need much; in this heat. Get up and try them on."

George was presently arrayed, like Loto in low, tight slippers of soft hide — clipped dog-skin, Loto told him — wide trousers of white material, bulging above the knees and tight at the ankles; and a brown and green cloth jacket, ornamented with little metal coins. The jacket was square-cut and short. It just covered the waist-band of the trousers in back. It had quaint, flaring sleeves that ended at the elbow. It was lined with something soft, thin and yet absorbent; and it felt smooth and comfortable next to George's skin. But it would not meet in front; it left George's chest and stomach bare. He stood regarding it ruefully until Loto showed him how to fasten it closed across his stomach.

"Nice and cool — when you get used to it," George commented, staring down at his exposed chest. "How do I look? Kind of queer, don't I?" He twisted himself around, trying to see down over the side bulge of his trousers.

Rogers' voice, calling, interrupted them.

"I've got a million things to talk to you about," George was telling Loto. "Hurry it up — I'll be out in the garden."

They met, a few minutes later, on the side veranda, where they were to have the morning meal. George's self-consciousness vanished immediately. Rogers was dressed almost exactly as he was — and he flattered himself he looked at least as well as his companion.

It seemed, to the new arrivals, at this first glance, a primitive world indeed into which they had fallen. The heat, the palms, the thatched bungalow, and their costumes — all might almost have existed in some out-of-the-way tropical land of their own time-world.

During the meal George was insistent with questions, but Loto smilingly refused to talk. Instead, he led his father into a brief description of their flight forward through time and south through space. When the meal was over Loto took them to the front veranda.

"I've a great deal to tell you," he said, "and I know you're as impatient to hear it as I am to have you. I've been here on the island five months —"

"We realize it," George murmured. "Didn't I watch for that light through every day and night of 'em?"

Loto smiled. "I put the signal up last night because I felt that I needed you. Before we do anything I must tell you of our affairs here. You notice I say 'our affairs.' They are a part of me now. I don't exactly know why, but the thing here grips me. I want to help these people — I feel already that I am one of them."

It was no mystery to George.

"Where's Azeela?" he demanded with apparent irrelevancy.

"In Anglese City — the capital and largest center of population on the island. It's north of here — on the channel. I've been living there. I came down here merely to meet you. The situation here is drastic, father. War has been impending, and now it will not be postponed much longer. This Toroh — as I told you, he is an Anglese renegade — is organizing the barbarians of the north — the *Noths*, as they are called. They are a people of low intelligence — brutes of men with black hair thick on their bodies.

"God knows how many of them there are — hordes scattered about the northern wastes of snow. Toroh has been gathering them. He has a base up north where he is manufacturing scientific weapons. There is class hatred here on the island, but, thank Heaven, in the face of an outside invasion, the Anglese will stick together."

"You're preparing for war," George interposed. "You —"

"Yes, of course. The Anglese have had no warfare for several generations. They were totally unprepared. But now they are getting things in shape."

Loto's tone was optimistic, but the anxiety of his expression belied it. "I wanted you here, father — you and George. Without Toroh, we would not fear the Noths. But Toroh is a scientist; and what weapons he will have been able to manufacture we do not know. We can only —"

The figure of a man came dashing up the garden path — a man in the familiar wide trousers, torn and dirty. His red-brown, naked torso gleamed with sweat; a white cloth was tied about his forehead to keep the damp hair from his eyes.

Loto leaped to his feet; and the man, gazing at the strangers with one swift, surprised glance, flung himself prostrate on the steps.

"What —" began Rogers.

"Wait! A messenger from Azeela. Something has gone wrong."

Loto raised the man up, and listened to his flood of frightened words with obvious concern. A sharp question from Loto — a crisp order — and the messenger was dashing away. Loto's gaze, following him, came back to his companions on the porch.

"Bad news, father. We must get up to Anglese City at once. Spies have appeared in Orleen — a city at the western end of the island — spies from Toroh, former Anglese, banished like himself. They are being put to death as fast as they can be caught. But meanwhile they are talking to the lower class — telling the people that Toroh is for them, and only against their government. There is class hatred here. The people are listening to the emissaries. We may be facing a revolution — an internal break, on the eve of fighting the Noths! We will lose if that happens — lose to Toroh inevitably!"

CHAPTER XIV.

"AFTER US — THE DELUGE!"

THEY were down on the beach in five minutes more. The plane stood there undisturbed. Half a dozen figures rose from the sand beside it and stood respectfully waiting for Loto to approach.

Rogers took his seat beside the Frazia controls. They were presently in the air, flying northward over the palm-covered island that lay calm, serene in its false security and peacefulness.

Loto sat close to his father, with George beside them.

"I must tell you briefly the conditions here," Loto said. "Then you will be able to understand — be able to help with your advice and judgment as well as actions."

He spoke briskly, but carefully, and his manner regained its poise. George was gazing down through one of the side windows.

"That's Azeela's messenger," Loto commented, "going back to Anglese City."

174

They were flying hardly five hundred feet above the palms. A white road lay beneath them. Along it a huge, shaggy dog was running, with the figure of a man on its back. The dog's neck was stretched forward, its body low to the ground as it ran with almost incredible speed, the man lashing its flanks with a leather thong. The plane passed very slowly and drew away.

"We will not land in the heart of the city," Loto added. "He'll be with Azeela before we are."

"Go on and tell us about things," George urged. "We've got the time now; maybe we won't have it later."

Loto nodded. "I will. We have here on the island three social classes. How they developed throughout the centuries you will have to imagine for yourself. Ancient, almost prehistoric Egypt was no more than a quarter as far into the past of our time-world as we are now ahead of it. Considered in that light, the changes have been rather less radical than you would anticipate.

"The lowest class — you would call them peons in our old Latin America — are now termed the *Bas*.

175

They include more than nine-tenths of all the inhabitants of the island. Most of them are ignorant, uneducated; yet they include, also, many intelligent learned individuals.

"It is the lowest class which is now plunged into almost intolerable conditions. They are the workers — red-brown skinned from the sun through generations. The higher class — the nobility — are the *Arans*. They are the governing class; they live for the most part in idleness and luxury — while the Bas are held down to almost universal poverty.

"You have not seen the Arans yet. We will shortly be in their chief city. You will find them white-skinned — their women especially, milk white, for they shield themselves carefully from the sun. They are cultured, yet without great learning. Can you appreciate that condition? It is they who really show the decadence of this time-world."

"There is a third class," Rogers prompted.

"Yes. The scientists — to me the most interesting of all. You will appreciate that in long past ages, science was supreme. In war it was everything. The Anglese came to this island — grew apathetic.

But the scientists, in some measure, clung to their learning. Gradually, their attitude must have changed to secrecy. They became a sect, holding knowledge for its own sake, keeping it among themselves.

"The real power lay with them, and they knew it. But curiously enough, their science seemed all-sufficient. As a body, they never desired governing power—no individual rose among them with a yearning for conquest, except Toroh.

"Foreign wars came. The scientists offered their help—and when the wars were over, retired with their knowledge to themselves. The sect, as you will find it to-day, is on the down grade. It has dwindled to a thousand or two individuals—no more—who are scattered throughout the island. They call themselves the League—I should say, a word that means about that. They have their own officers—a council of a hundred in Anglese City, and a life-time president, Fahn, Azeela's father.

"Thus, you understand, the League of Scientists really controls everything. But its members are content with the prestige their position gives them. The government itself has for centuries fostered this secrecy of all that pertains to science. In times of war, the Arans are helpless, and leave it all to the League. In times of peace they forget the possibility of war and go back to ruling the Bas in their own fashion."

Loto glanced out one of the windows. "Look down there."

The island was mountainous — a constant succession of green hills and valleys. A small lake came into view, with steam rising from it. Everywhere the scene was dotted with thatched huts — occasionally a more pretentious bungalow like the one in which the visitors had passed the previous night. As they flew low over the hills, they could see small brown and white patches of cultivated areas scattered everywhere.

"That is the way the Bas live," Loto commented. "Sometimes they bring their produce to the cities and sell it for sums ridiculously small. If there is a food shortage, the Arans come out and take it — paying for it nominally."

"But your factories — your industries?"

"In the cities, father. Reduced to a minimum —

for the use and welfare of the Arans and scientists almost exclusively. Skilled labor is performed by the higher types of the Bas. They are allowed to live in the cities — but are paid so little that they must live unpretentiously. Everything is done for the welfare of the Arans — and the League of Scientists."

"And the government?"

"A monarchy. A king and his council of fifty — and his personal cabinet of five. A hereditary monarch, wholly inefficient, except in forcing his laws upon the Bas."

"I should think that would be somewhat difficult," Rogers commented.

"No, sir. There is a large police force — swaggering young men of the Arans. They serve for the joy of it — they're most arrogant individuals who take pleasure in the enforcement of the personal power they hold. And they abuse it, of course. Their task is easy, for they have the scientists behind them. Any one of them killed, or even attacked by a Bas, would mean the death of that Bas and all his family.

" I said the Bas were under conditions almost intolerable. And that's exactly why these spies of Toroh's are dangerous to us just now. The whole social condition here is wretched — yet, I suppose, logical enough under the circumstances of environment and racial development. Fundamentally, the difficulty has been a limited land area. The race cannot expand, hence numerically it must be restrained."

" How? " demanded Rogers. " By birth control? "

" Yes, sir. Obligatory birth control. Applicable only to the Bas. More Bas are not desired, hence births are limited. The desire just now — more than to hold the population even — is to cut it down. Hence, a Bas woman is allowed but two offspring."

" But suppose she has three? " George suggested.

" The mother and her child — illegitimate in a new sense — are banished from the island." Loto's voice rose to sudden vehemence. " Can you understand what that sometimes does? I have seen a mother with her newborn infant, two or three weeks old, pleading before the King's Council. She would not murder it at birth, as the Bas women sometimes

180

do; and I saw her plead for its right to live on the island. And then, with her plea denied, she took it away into the frozen north. Her husband did not follow her. That is optional. This one stayed behind, keeping the other two children, and letting her take the infant alone. And she went, to save its life—her child, born without a birthright."

There was a silence. Rogers was staring down at a hilltop, where, as the plane swept past, a woman with two naked children at her side stood in front of a small shack.

"And when you have seen the Arans, living their life of luxury and immorality," Loto went on, "you will wonder why the Bas have stood it so long. 'After us—the deluge.' That has always been the Aran reasoning."

The plane was climbing to pass over a jagged, volcanic-looking peak. Behind it, nestled in a hollow, with a curving stretch of white sand and the blue waters of the channel beyond, lay the capital city of the Arans—reckless, pleasure-loving, secure in its beauty and supremacy, yet trembling from so many causes upon the brink of disaster.

181

CHAPTER XV.

THE SCIENTIST AND HIS DAUGHTERS.

Oᴺ the gently undulating floor of a valley, surrounded by three mountains and with the sea rolling up on its beach to the north, lay the Aran city. From an altitude of some three thousand feet, the travelers gazed down upon a scene of extraordinary color and beauty. Low buildings of pure white — buildings with many balconies and patios with tiny fountains; gardens of vivid flowers; white pergolas trellised with scarlet blossoms; sunken pools of limpid water, with huge date-palms curving over them. A grove of royal palms close to the beach, with a huge, rectangular bathing pool and a white pavilion beside it. A white palace stood on a rise of ground with a balconied tower, five hundred feet high, beside it, on the top a beautiful flower garden. And everywhere the romantic green foliage of the tropics, the blue-red sky, soft red-white clouds, and the azure channel.

"Where do we land?" George asked.

"To the west a little, father," Loto directed. "See the cavern entrance?"

He pointed for George, explaining: "We will not land directly in the city. I want the plane permanently guarded now. We will leave it with my plane — in the Cavern of Thunderbolts."

"The what?" George demanded.

"That's what the Bas picturesquely call it. You see the cavern mouth?"

Across the city a yawning black hole gaped in the mountainside near its base — an opening of irregularly circular shape some two hundred feet in diameter. A gentle slope led up to it from the city. It seemed the gigantic mouth of a cave.

"We can fly directly in," Loto added. "It is the entrance to the subterranean chambers where the scientists work — and where they store their apparatus under guard. It is a museum also, where relics of the past are gathered."

George relapsed into an awed silence, staring down at the city. In the city streets now, and on the housetops, figures were standing, gazing up at the plane curiously.

The mouth of the cavern grew steadily larger as the plane swooped down upon it. The yawning hole seemed to have a level floor extending horizontally back into the mountain. Far back into the darkness little blue lights twinkled.

"You'd better take the controls, Loto," Rogers said anxiously. "I don't like the idea of flying into that—at some fifty miles an hour."

Loto slipped quietly into the seat and relieved him. The Frazia motors stopped abruptly. Silently, with only the sound of the air rushing past, the plane glided swiftly downward.

About the cavern mouth was a small platform with a roof over it, built on an overhanging ledge of rock. The figures of three men seated there were visible. Abruptly one of the figures rose, and from its upflung hand a tiny flash of blue-white light shot into the clouds overhead. Even in the daylight it was a plainly visible flash.

"Lightning!" exclaimed George; and as though to confirm him, a little miniature crack of thunder sounded an instant later.

"They know I'm coming," Loto said.

184

It was a queer sensation, darting into that blackness. The cave mouth seemed to open and swallow them. The plane struck the ground with a bump, lifted, bumped again, and rolled forward. Points of light swept past on either side; a blue-white glare lay ahead. Dark figures were moving about in it.

The plane slackened its speed and came to a stop.

"We're here," said Loto. "Take only what you will need at once. We can come back here later to-day or to-morrow."

They were soon on the clay ground. The hum of dynamos sounded from far away in the mountain's depths. The roof high overhead was dimly visible. Ledges on the side walls held black holes behind them. Great shadows, flickering blue-white lights, were everywhere. Near at hand was a space more brightly lighted—where the cave broadened—and narrowed again beyond, with a dozen branching passages. An incline fifty feet broad sloped down into blackness, with a faint pencil-point of blue light shining far down within its recesses.

"Why, the whole mountain is honeycombed!" Rogers exclaimed.

"Yes, sir. Just a minute and I'll be with you. Stand still! Don't move about!"

Figures were approaching, robed in black rubber garments, gloved and hooded. Loto turned to greet them, and they drew back their hoods, disclosing the heads and faces of men. There was a brief conversation, then Loto turned back to his companions.

"Fahn is at home in the city," he said swiftly, and his tone was concerned. "We'll go."

The black-robed figures gazed at them curiously a moment; then went back to their work. Led by Loto, the three started off toward the mouth of the cave, which showed small and bright in the darkness.

"Is your plane in here, Loto?" Rogers asked.

"No, sir. I left it at Orleen. There is a cavern there similar to this — but smaller. It's there — in the other cavern."

"You're sure it's safe?"

"Yes, father. Of course."

"Where are we going?" George demanded after a moment.

"To Fahn's home," answered Loto. "He'll be there — with Azeela and Dianne."

"Dianne?" George's voice was thrilled. "Who is that?"

"Azeela's younger sister," Loto explained briefly. He smiled. "I meant to tell you about her, George. She's a little dare-devil. You'll like her."

George did not answer, and for some time they walked on in silence. The ground was wet, like muddy clay. There were no lights ahead, no figures; but the daylight from the cave's mouth lighted their way.

They passed out of the cave and on to a road of white sand and clay that led down the mountain slope. Palms lined it thickly. Further down, at the bottom of the quarter-mile descent, houses began — the outskirts of the city. The road soon took on the aspect of a street. It was broad, with narrow pedestrian paths on both sides. Flower gardens, often with hedges of thick, bayonet-like plants, lined the paths. The houses were for the most part almost obscured by palms and trellised vines that were loaded with scarlet blossoms. Private outdoor bathing pools occasionally showed among the garden foliage.

It was obviously a residential section. As the party advanced, passers-by grew more numerous. The Bas men were distinguishable by their clipped, bullet-like heads, covered with broad, circular-brimmed hats of straw, their sun-tanned bodies naked above the waist, bare feet, and the wide trousers; and the Bas women, red-brown of skin as well, clothed usually merely with a loin cloth and a white sash bound over the breasts, their hair twisted in plaits hanging down the back.

The Bas walked always in the road itself. On the pedestrian paths occasional Arans passed — men with hair long to the base of the neck, and dressed somewhat as Loto had garbed his father and friend. Most of them saluted Loto — a queer, flowing gesture of the left hand — and all of them stared with frank curiosity at the strangers. Occasionally an Aran woman came along — white swathed, mysterious figures — a twinkle of tiny, black-slippered feet — a flash from alluring eyes veiled by lashes heavily darkened.

An Aran man riding a dog went slowly by down a cross street. A dog pulling a small three-wheeled cart piled high with merchandise passed in the opposite direction.

George edged toward Loto. "Those dogs," he whispered. "They're friendly? Not vicious?"

"Of course not," Loto laughed. "Just like regular dogs. Except — well, I'll tell you later."

George sighed with relief. "All right. But they're not like any dog I ever saw at home. They're nearly as big as a horse. And there's something else wrong about them — they're too intelligent. You can see that just by looking at them walk."

Presently they turned into the gateway of a hedge solid with white and scarlet blossoms.

"Fahn's home," Loto said. "We'll go right in."

George went forward to walk with Loto. They passed through a garden, colorful with its mass of vivid flowers, and heavy with the languorous scent of magnolia and orange blossoms. The house stood well back from the road. It was a white house, low and broad. George got an impression of smooth white columns that looked almost like marble, but were wood; a few steps; a low-hanging roof — not thatched, but seemingly of blue tiling.

Then they were on the veranda. The walls of the house sloped inward at the top. There was a window nearby — no glass — but with a blue-white silky curtain shrouding it. The doorway stood open. George could see a hall, with another open door to the sunlight of a patio banked with flowers.

A girl came to the doorway. It was Azeela. George knew her at once — a slight little creature of blue eyes, golden hair and milk-white skin; a pale blue silky sash wound wide about her hips and thighs, breastplates of metal, with the broad, circular collar above them, and her hair parted forward over her shoulders in plaits that ended with little tassels. George thought her the most beautiful girl he had ever seen; Loto's description did not half do her justice.

She stood hesitantly in the doorway; then, smiling, advanced to Loto and gave him her two hands with a pretty gesture of welcome.

George's impression that Azeela was the prettiest girl he had ever seen was short lived, for behind Azeela now came another girl — her younger sister, Dianne. Azeela might have been eighteen or nineteen; Dianne obviously was no more than sixteen — a black-haired, dark-eyed girl, dressed like Azeela, except that her sash was a deep red.

George's heart was beating furiously as he acknowledged the introductions.

"And this is Dianne," Loto said. "We call her Dee."

"So will I," said George promptly. He met the girl's eyes — snapping, laughing eyes with the spirit of deviltry in them.

"Loto told me about you," she said demurely. Her intonation was that of a foreigner, but she spoke the Ancient English with perfect ease and fluency. "Loto said he thought I would like you a lot."

"He didn't tell me about *you*," George responded. "Not till ten minutes ago. But, anyway, he was right. No, what I mean is —"

The rest of George's speech was lost, for they were inside the house and Fahn was advancing to meet them. The leader of the scientists was a man of nearly seventy — a quiet, grave, dominating figure, tall and spare, but perfectly erect. His face was smooth-shaven; his iron-gray hair he wore long to the base of the neck. He was dressed in a paneled robe of black, with white ruching at his wrists and throat.

"I am glad, indeed, to have you with us," he said cordially to Rogers. He spoke precisely, slowly and carefully, as one speaks a language newly mastered. "I feel very close to you, now that my daughter Azeela is to marry Loto. It makes me —"

Rogers stared blankly. "Loto engaged? Why, Loto, you —"

"There was so much else to tell you, father." Loto was covered with confusion. "Besides, I wanted to have you meet Azeela first."

Azeela was trying to escape from the room; but Dee captured her and pushed her back.

George was vigorously congratulating Loto; and Rogers, rising to the occasion, kissed Azeela heartily.

CHAPTER XVI.

BLOOD OF THE MOON.

IT was an ominous crisis into which the visitors from a time world twenty-eight thousand years previous had fallen. They discussed it with Fahn and his daughters during the remainder of that morning, and at the light noon meal, served in a shaded corner of the patio formed by the enclosing wings of the house. Banks of vivid flowers surrounded them; the quiet, warm air was redolent with perfume. A small fountain splashed musically. The world was calm, languorous.

Fahn had little to add to what they already knew. Toroh and the Noths had not been expected to attack for a month or two at least, and the Anglese scientists were going forward with their own preparations for the war with the utmost haste.

But now these emissaries Toroh had smuggled to the island injected a new and alarming factor into the situation. They had appeared only in Orleen.

But the Bas were listening to them; and all over the island the news was spreading among the Bas that Toroh was a friend — not an enemy. The Bas might be incited to open revolt.

"Mogruud is alarmed," Fahn said to Loto. He explained to the others that Mogruud was one of the most intelligent of the Bas in Anglese City — a leader of them. Mogruud was not fooled by Toroh's emissaries. But he feared now that he could not control his people.

"And the most terrible part is the Bas are right," Fahn added. "I do not mean in regard to Toroh — *he* is a scoundrel, of course. But the Bas must have some relief. Their children — ten mothers and infants were ordered exiled yesterday."

"Why don't you fix it?" George exclaimed.

The scientist leader shrugged slightly. "I do not make the laws. I obey them. I have remonstrated with the king and the council many times." He paused, then added thoughtfully:

"The time may come when we of the league may be forced to act against the laws of our king. He is wrong, and we scientists all know it. But to take the law into our own hands—it is a very drastic thing—"

During the meal, George was far more interested in the two sisters than in the men's talk. He had opportunity now to study the girls, compare them. In feature they were much alike—in expression and demeanor, totally different. Azeela was calm, thoughtful and femininely sweet. Dee was impulsive, vivacious—alternately demure and devilish, as George phrased it to himself. Yet, in spite of the difference in temperament, there seemed a strange bond between the sisters. Their regard for each other—the love between them—was obvious. But it was more than that—a bond of the mind and spirit. George puzzled over it. Often when Azeela was about to speak, Dee would impulsively speak for her—as though interpreting her sister's thoughts.

The afternoon was one of inactivity. A Toroh emissary appeared in Anglese City, but he was arrested before he had time to harangue the people.

"I had thought him one of Toroh's brothers," Fahn remarked. "But it is not so. I think now they would not dare come back to the island."

195

He went on to explain that Toroh had two younger brothers, banished like himself.

"They might come — Toroh himself m i g h t come," Loto declared. "He will dare anything that seems worth the risk."

"If we take any one of them he will die," Fahn commented.

It was at this juncture, in the late afternoon when the whole world was bathed in the glorious colors of a sunset sky, that Azeela returned from a short trip across the city.

"The Aran Festival of the Flowers is tonight," she exclaimed excitedly. "It has not been postponed. The Arans say it is clever to hold it now, in spite of the news from Orleen. It will show the Bas how little they care — how secure is the Aran power!"

It seemed to presage evil events — the holding of this festival wherein all the wanton luxury of the Arans could be flaunted in the face of those whom they ruled; and with foreboding in their hearts, Fahn, his daughters and their friends, prepared that evening to go and witness it. Midnight was at hand when they started. Dee and Azeela were swathed to the eyes in soft white robes; and the men carried in their hands tiny black masks.

The city streets, even at midnight, bore a holiday aspect. The moon had risen; but in addition to its light, there was above every street crossing a brazier hanging on wires, which cast a soft blue light downward.

Arans were hurrying along, alone and in groups —the women all shrouded in white; the men, in clothes of gaudy colors, wearing masks, or dangling them in their hands. Little phaetons drawn by dogs rolled by, filled with gay figures in fancy dress —women leaning from them with a flash of white arms and neck and face, waving at the pedestrians and tossing out flowers as they swept past.

Loto and Azeela, with George and Dee close behind them, led the way swiftly in the direction that every one else was moving. Fahn and Rogers followed them.

It was a fairylike city of unreality. Gaudy shapes of men and white robed women hastening forward under the blue street lights; silent white houses back from the street, with somnolent gardens drowsing in the moonlight, pale and wan and yet flushed a little with the reddish tinge of the moon; warm, moist air, almost without a breath, heavy with sensuous perfume.

And in the shadows of the streets, the brown skinned, half naked figure of a Bas, skulking here and there!

Azeela had for some time been walking in silence. She looked up at the moon and with a touch upon Loto's arm, indicated it.

"You said the moon was blushing, my Loto — the rose blush of maiden modesty to look down upon such a city. But I do not see it so. To me it is stained with blood."

The sweeping gesture of her white arm from under the robe went to a garden beside them.

"Blood, beloved — staining everything!"

The street topped a rise of ground; ahead, down another short slope, lay the sea. And even there the silver path upon the water was tinged with red.

CHAPTER XVII.

DECADENCE.

A CORDON of police stopped Fahn and his party at the edge of a grove of palms near the beach. A moment more and they were inside. It was dim under the palms — the white sand a lace pattern of shadow and moonlight. Gay figures were moving about, all the men masked now.

The grove was perhaps a quarter of a mile in extent. To the right lay the gleaming white beach with the surf rolling up upon it. A tremendous pile of scarlet and white blossoms stood near by under the palm trees. Figures rushed to it, gathered up armfuls and darted away, shouting and laughing.

"We must keep together," said Fahn. "Come this way."

Half a dozen men had whirled up, pelting Azeela and Dee with flower blossoms, and under cover of the laughing attack, trying to separate one of them from their escorts and carry her off.

199

They moved slowly forward, George gripping Dee's arm tightly. They passed a huge, rectangular swimming pool, deserted as yet — glassy, moonlit water a foot or two below the surface of the ground, reflecting the dark outlines of the date palms that curved above it.

The whirling crowd constantly became denser. There must have been several thousand people within the grove; the white shrouded figure of a woman flinging flowers against the attack of a man; a woman retreating, with ammunition exhausted, to the flower pile to replenish, and being caught in a smothering embrace before she could reach it; a group of laughing girls with robes torn from them in the fray, pelting a defenseless man, flinging him finally into a huge pile of flower petals, burying him until some other quarry distracted their attention, or until a stronger force of men separated them, sometimes carrying them off bodily.

And there were nooks behind hedges of flowers — stolen embraces of couples, alone until marauding bands of men or girls found them out and drove them from their seclusion.

The white sand in places was thick with trampled flowers. Music came drifting through the warm night air — music near at hand, but blurred by the shouts of the whirling throng. The rich contralto voice of a woman singing — a snatch broken off into laughter.

A large white pavilion lay ahead, brilliant with flashing colored lights — a kaleidoscope of shifting color. It seemed crowded with people, and toward it Fahn now led his little party.

They did not enter the pavilion, but stood in a group on its white steps. The music came from within — music that welled and throbbed, unfamiliar in character, but with the age-old appeal to the senses — music sensuous, barbaric. And yet was it barbaric?

Rogers voiced the question in a whisper to Loto, who stood beside him. Was it not rather super-modern, with the centuries of decadence that had put into it that fire of the soul abandoned to the body?

The throng on the floor was battling with flowers, drinking wine from carved bowls of coconut shell, and dancing indiscriminately. The masked men, many of them, were robed in black; the women shrouded in white. But the swinging lights of vivid color stained everything and made the scene shift and blur into fantasy.

At one end of the room a huge circular table was loaded with food and drink, fruits and confections. The table was slowly revolving; half of its circumference was behind a partition — a kitchen where it was constantly being replenished with other dainties.

The visitors found it difficult to keep their place on the pavilion steps; masked men attacked the two girls with flowers; a black robed figure in mock politeness and humility begged one or the other of them to dance. A trio of girls tore George away, and then at his fierce resistance, left him abruptly.

"The king," whispered Loto, with a gesture.

At one end of the pavilion on a small raised platform the king sat smiling down upon the scene. He was robed in paneled cloth of rich, gaudy colors — a man of middle age whose long, dark hair was shot through with gray.

The scene, with its confusion of shifting incident, held too much for the visitors to see or to understand. Half an hour went by, with the merrymaking steadily increasing. Abruptly the music, which had been continuous, was stilled. The throng stopped in its tracks, waiting expectantly. The swinging colored lights died out; others took their place—pure blue-white, and motionless. A solemn bell tolled out over the silence; with almost one motion the masks and the robes were discarded. A woman's laugh, that carried in it the very essence of abandonment, rang out; then the music began; the throng sprang again into motion.

The riotous color had been of light; now with the light a blue-white, steady glare, it was the riotous color of costume. To George it was Bagdad of the Ancients—manikins, with turbaned headdresses, and flowing vivid draperies with the gleaming white of limbs beneath them. Or were these slave girls, with their wares held to the gaze of the bidders in the market? Circassian slaves, white of body. Or these others—desert women, dancing with a pagan lust?

203

George's impressions were confused. Yet the thought came to him that it was not like any of those. It was modern beyond his time — decadence, not barbarism.

Again Rogers murmured something of the kind, but his words were lost. A score of figures came leaping from the pavilion scattering the small group of onlookers on its steps.

Rogers recovered himself, turning to follow them with his gaze — white nymphs with flowing hair, and draperies of gauze that fell from them as they ran for the moonlit beach and the surf.

Loto, pulling at his father's arm, brought his attention back to the pavilion. Through it, the palm-grove on the other side was visible.

The bathing pool was now a turmoil of splashing figures — slim white shapes dove into it from the palm-lined banks.

But Loto was indicating the pavilion's interior. The crowd was standing motionless, gazing upward. A small dais was poised in mid-air above the floor in the center of the room. It floated there, seemingly with nothing to sustain it. Standing on tiptoe on the dais was the figure of a woman wrapped to the eyes in scarlet draperies. She was facing the king over a distance of some twenty feet. The music, which had been stilled for a moment, murmured softly from its unseen niche.

Fahn whispered to Rogers: "Our workmen of the League equipped that dais for the king. He begged us — and I feel now that it was a mistake."

Loto added: "It is made from our newly invented war equipment. The dais is covered with a fabric — electrically charged, and repulsive to the earth. It is radio controlled, father. A workman from the cavern is over there in the corner, behind that portiere. We have kept the fabric a secret — but the king wanted to use it for the dais."

The woman was singing — a throbbing contralto — very soft at first, then gradually louder. As she sang, slowly she unwound the draperies, letting them drop from her like quivering flame to a smoldering pile at her feet. Beneath were other draperies, flame-colored like the rest, but her arms and face were bare — full, rounded arms milk-white — a heavy face with scarlet lips.

"Helene," Loto whispered. "The Bas call her what means 'Mme. Voluptua.' It is she who rules this king and this nation. Look at her!"

The king was standing up. The music grew louder, fiercer, with a thrilling minor cadence. The woman's arms were extended; she stood poised, smiling as she sang to the king. From her outflung arms the gauze drapery hung like quivering wings; the white of her body gleamed beneath it; the black hair piled on her head held two trembling spangles of gold at the end of golden wires. She stood, a great scarlet moth, hovering before flight.

Staring in fascination, the king had left his seat and descended to the floor. The crowd parted to make way for him as he slowly moved toward the dais which floated down to meet him. Every eye was on him and on the woman, who now was extending her arms down in invitation.

The music and the song were at their height. The dais reached the floor; the king stepped upon it and as the woman's hand touched his shoulder, he dropped on one knee before her, his lips to the hem of her scarlet gauze.

A leer of triumph on the woman's face; a murmur of applause from the watching throng. Then a black cloak fell from a figure close beside the dais; a man leaped upon it — the naked figure of a man in loin-cloth. A knife flashed — blue-white steel in the light from above. The song turned to a shuddering scream. The scarlet figure wilted and sank among its draperies at the feet of the kneeling king!

CHAPTER XVIII.

THE GUILT WITHIN THEM.

FOR an instant the colorful throng seemed frozen, then chaos — the struggling, aimless confusion of panic. The murderer had flung the king and the body of the woman from the dais. The little platform was rising into the air, carrying him with it. The movement was sidewise; in a moment it would have been outside the pavilion.

Rogers, standing beside Fahn, heard the Scientist leader mutter an oath. Fahn's hand came up from his robe; a pencil-point of flame — a tiny shaft, yellow-red — shot from his weapon. The platform crashed to the floor of the pavilion; the murderer lay still, his body blackened and charred.

In the center of the room, the king had climbed to his feet, trembling, staring down at the scarlet pile of gauze before him — the crumbled white body stained red as the draperies in which it lay.

The pavilion was emptying. The music was

stilled; shouts of men; terrified, hysterical cries of women filled the air. The visitors on the steps were swept back by the press from within. Loto, clinging to his father, struggled to hold them together.

From the beach white figures were running away; slim shapes were climbing from the bathing pool. A woman hastened by, long black hair plastered wet against her sleek white body; her face, with the sex allure gone from it, was a white mask of horror; a scarlet mouth with lips parted to yield babbling, terrified cries. She swept past and disappeared into the confusion of the moonlit night.

Loto was still clutching his father; all the rest of their party had disappeared. The pavilion now was empty of Arans, save for that huddled scarlet form, deserted by all its kind.

Fahn came hastening up. "That is one of Toroh's brothers." He pointed to the motionless figure of the man his jet of flame had killed. "The other brother murdered my operator. They planned to steal the fabric—to duplicate it and use it against us in the war. I had no idea they would dare come to the island."

Fahn had found his radio operator lying dead in his place behind the portiere. Toroh's other brother had been there — trying to use the radio — to get the dais out of the pavilion so that in the confusion they might escape with it. Fahn had caught a glimpse of the man running away as he approached. They had not known of Fahn's presence at the festival; had he not been there, the attempt probably would have succeeded.

There was space around the three men now; the fleeing Aran figures were vanishing through the palms; the confused cries were growing fainter. But George and the two girls could not be found.

"We must go back," said Fahn. "They must have tried to find us and could not. They would go home at once."

With a last search around them, the three men started off through the now almost deserted grove. The cordon of police had disappeared. A few hastening figures were scattered in the distance along the streets.

"Come," said Loto anxiously. "We must hurry."

Keeping close together they hastened along. Aran

figures scurried here and there; lights twinkled in the houses, then were extinguished as though the concealing darkness might offer protection.

"Curious," murmured Rogers, "the entire city is in terror."

"The guilt that has been within them for generations," Fahn answered. "Toroh planned this well. The Bas will not know it was an attempt to steal the fabric. They will think it merely that one of their own people dared to murder Mme. Voluptua. The Arans think that now. They think the Bas have risen to rebellion at last. It is not this one murder, but the meaning of it that they fear — the confidence it will give the Bas."

And as though to confirm his words, the figure of a Bas man stood motionless on the next street corner. He was partly in shadow, but he did not move as the three men came along; and as they passed, his body seemed to straighten, with the consciousness of his own power sweeping over it.

Across the city they hurried. As they advanced, other Bas were seen — Bas who no longer skulked in the shadows.

211

At last they came to the shimmering, moonlit garden of Fahn's home. The house was dark. They called, but no one answered. A brief search revealed the truth; about the house or the grounds, Azeela, George and Dee were not to be found. The place was undisturbed; there seemed no evidence of marauders.

"We must wait," said Fahn. But his tone was anxious. "They have not yet arrived from the grove. I cannot believe it is anything but that."

For a time they waited, but none of the missing three appeared. A hum had been growing in the city — a murmur of distant cries that now forced itself on their attention. The murmur grew, resolved itself into shouts and the scuffle of running feet. Around a street corner near by a mob of Bas appeared and swept past the house. The crowd might have held a thousand persons. A giant, half-naked man with a curving sword-blade in his hand was leading, running, grimly silent; behind him came many brown-skinned men and women — the men, most of them with curving swords, the women with sticks, the heavy butts of palm-fronds with the green stripped off, and a variety of agricultural implements seized and now to be used as weapons.

"The cane-cutters!" Loto exclaimed softly. "The knives with which they cut the sugar cane. They —"

He broke off, watching the mob as with vainglorious shouts from a few, but most grimly silent, it swept by. At every corner it was strengthened by others who joined it; Bas were springing up miraculously from the shadows everywhere.

Fahn's hand had gone to his belt; then it dropped to his side. Rogers met the Scientist's glance with a nod of understanding.

"It is what we of the League have feared for years," Fahn said anxiously. "I cannot kill my own people. I am armed, and they are not — yet I cannot kill them — cannot look upon them as enemies. And I think, even in their frenzy, they realize that and play upon it."

The last stragglers had passed; the shouts of the mob were growing fainter as it dashed across the city. The Aran houses were still dark and silent, with only an occasional inmate slinking out to gaze fearfully around. Directly across the street the white figure of a woman just returned from the grove showed for an instant in a doorway. Then it fled inward, into the darkness.

"The palace!" said Loto abruptly. "They're going to the palace!"

The words seemed to bring to Fahn the realization that action by him was needed. For the moment his anxiety over his daughters became secondary.

"Come!" he exclaimed. "We must protect the king."

He hurried them through the garden and along the street. Almost running, the three men headed toward where the mob could still be heard, shouting in the distance.

CHAPTER XIX.

NEW DISASTER.

GEORGE had been standing with his friends beside
the pavilion, silently watching the festival
reach its height. The bell tolled; the masks and
cloaks were discarded. A bevy of nymphs with
flowing gauze draperies came dashing out. As they
passed, one of them caught George by the arm,
pulling him along a few steps; her eyes, half hidden
by her tumbling hair, mocked him provocatively.

George jerked away. A tide of other figures
flowed from the pavilion, following the nymphs to
the beach. George fought his way back. He must
rejoin his friends; in that crowd they could get lost
so easily.

He was looking about, wondering just where they
had been standing before, when he saw Dee. Her
white cloak had fallen from her head to her shoulders. She was standing alone, apparently lost in
reverie.

George hastened to her. "Where are —"

But her vehement gesture silenced him; again she seemed lost in thought. For a moment he stood wondering what was the matter with her. The music from the pavilion throbbed out into the moon-lit grove; all around them the gayety was surging.

Finally George could stand it no longer. "Dee, what is it? What's the matter?"

She looked up with an anxious frown. "Something is wrong. With Azeela. She's trying to tell me what's wrong."

"Oh!" George glanced hastily about. "Where is Azeela? She was here a minute ago. Where are the rest of them? Let's tell them."

What did Dee mean? The girl seemed to have forgotten him again. She was moving slowly away, like one who walks under a spell.

"Wait. Oh, Dee — wait a minute!"

She kept on going. Figures were passing between them now. George hated to leave his place. He'd never find the others — never get back again. Even now he realized it would be difficult if not impossible to find them in all that crowd of masked figures. If he lost Dee, too— He had no choice; he darted after Dee.

When he had overtaken her they were some distance from the pavilion. It was more secluded here. George darted up and caught her by the arm.

"Dee! What's the matter with you?"

Her hand went over her eyes and she shook herself slightly. "It's hard at first—getting Azeela's thoughts. I have them now." She spoke swiftly, anxiously. "Toroh was here—a moment ago. He seized Azeela—he has taken her out of the grove —right near here."

Azeela's thoughts! George understood. He started forward; but she held him.

"Too late! Toroh had two dogs waiting for him. They are mounting them now. He has tied Azeela. They're starting—the dogs are running."

George stared at her blankly. "Where to? Where is he taking her? Can you ask her that? Can she tell you?"

The girl was hastening forward now, with George after her. "Yes. She says to Orleen. I have told her we are coming."

217

Abruptly she stopped and faced him. "George, we have two dogs at home. Shall you and I get them and go after Azeela?"

"Yes," he exclaimed impulsively.

"And I know where father keeps his weapons."

"Good. We can't find Loto and your father in this crowd. Had we better try, Dee?"

They were hurrying forward again.

"No," she said. "We'd lose too much time. Father forbade me touching his weapons," she added as an afterthought, "but this is different, isn't it?"

"Yes," he agreed excitedly. "You know how to work them, Dee?"

"Yes. I experimented. He doesn't know it."

They left the grove.

"Dee, where's Azeela now?"

"Crossing the city. West toward Orleen. We won't be far behind them."

George was trembling with the excitement of it. "Is Toroh armed? Ask Azeela that."

"I did. She doesn't know. She thinks he is."

"Oh!"

"We'll do something. He won't know we're after him — that's our advantage. Hurry, George!"

There were a few figures in the almost deserted streets, but George and Dee did not notice them. She was telling him of this branch of science for which she and her sister were distinguished — this telepathy they had developed. Bound in a union of thought by an unusual devotion, they had perfected it; until now they could know, always vaguely, and, with effort, quite distinctly, what was in the other's mind.

"We mustn't waste any time getting started, Dee."

They had entered the silent garden of Fahn's home. The city behind them was humming with confusion now, but they did not hear it — did not know that a murder had just been committed at the festival.

Within the house, Dee went at once to her father's room. George waited. When she returned she held two weapons out for his inspection. One was a crescent of transparent metal, with a tiny wire connecting its horns and a black bone handle by which to grasp it. There was a firing mechanism on the handle. It was the projector of the ray which caused muscular paralysis — the weapon Bool had used against Loto in the house in the snow.

Dee described its operation briefly.

The other weapon was a small black globe the size of a man's fist. It also had a handle with a trigger; in the globe opposite was a tiny orifice like the muzzle of a revolver. This was one of the smallest models of the thunderbolt projectors. With it a bolt of electrons could be thrown over a distance of some twenty feet.

The former weapon Dee kept; the little thunderbolt globe she handed to George.

Dee had discarded her white robe; a blue silken ribbon band around her forehead held the hair from her eyes. She had another in her hand; she tied it around George's head.

"It's hot riding, even at night," she explained. "Your hair gets moist — gets in your eyes."

They had been delayed only a moment.

"This way," she added.

They ran outside, across the patio, through a dark room and into the garden behind the house, where a small white outbuilding stood. A new misgiving overcame George.

"Oh, Dee—these dogs of yours—"

"You can ride a dog?" she asked back over her shoulder. Her expression was impish.

"I can ride anything," he said stoutly; but his tone was dubious. "If the dog is—"

She must have understood him, for she laughed. "Wait! You will find these dogs your friends."

George said nothing more, and in a moment they were within the kennel. It was dark, very dimly lighted by the moon form outside. A gray-black shape came toward them—a shaggy dog whose shoulders stood nearly as high as his own. George's whole instinct was to turn and run; but the dog padded up to Dee, and she put her arms up around it.

"Good, Rotan. Will you run fast for Dee?"

She called it toward George, and patted him to show the dog he was her friend. George impulsively put his hand up to the great shaggy neck, felt the dog's warm tongue as it turned to lick his hand. His perturbation vanished; this huge brute was his friend.

221

The other dog—Atal—was a male, larger than its mate; and standing beside it, George marveled at the power that its great body must hold. The dogs knew they were going out. They whined with eagerness, and leaping across the kennel, they came back to Dee with saddles in their mouths with which she was to harness them.

Rotan, which Dee was to ride, was saddled with a leather seat and a pommel with a small stirrup on one side. It was not unlike the side saddle for girls just before George's time. On Atal she strapped a thick leather pad with a stirrup on each side, on which he rode astride. There were no bridles.

"You tell Atal which way to go," she explained. "Right or left—slower or faster. Or if you want him to run or walk or stop, he will understand. Since Loto came we have taught them your way of saying it."

It all took no more than a moment or two, for Dee was hurrying, and her eagerness seemed to communicate to the dogs. They had barked at first —barks of such volume in the confined space that George was startled. But when Dee silenced them, they stood trembling with impatience, their heads turned to follow her as she adjusted the saddles.

George mounted Atal. It was almost like mounting a horse; and yet not like a horse either, for the dog's huge body under him was springy, supple. As it moved toward the doorway, George was reminded of the lithe grace and strength of a tiger. He missed the reins, and in lieu of them, twisted up two handfuls of hair on the dog's neck and clung.

Dee was ahead of him. "All right, George?"

"Right," he said confidently. "But we might as well take it slow—for a minute or two."

They moved silently through the garden. George leaned forward and down to the dog's face.

"Nice dog, Atal. You go slow till I tell you different. Understand?"

In the street, Dee was drawing away; and then Atal ran.

George clung desperately. But it was unnecessary. The dog's leaps were even and long; its padded paws as it hit the ground made no sound; its legs, all its muscles, seemed to give to the shock and absorb it.

They were running faster now; the dog's body seemed to settle closer to the ground; the wind whistled by George's ears. But he felt curiously secure. There was no question of the dog stumbling—falling; and its gait, now at a steady run, was far easier to ride than any horse he had ever mounted.

Dee was still ahead; the ends of the ribbon band about her head fluttered out behind her. The white road was a blur that swept beneath; the houses and gardens of the city were flying past.

An exhilaration—a feeling of triumph and power—came to George. He was perfectly at home on the dog's back now. This little Dee was a dare-devil, as Loto had said. Well, that was the sort of girl he liked. They'd overtake Toroh—kill him with a flash from the thunderbolt globes—rescue Azeela.

George leaned forward over the dog's neck.

"We might as well catch up with Dee," he said to the silky ear. "Faster, Atal!"

At once the dog increased its pace, overtaking its mate. At a run, side by side, they swept through the city.

To George the ride soon became a blur—a white moonlit road passing under him, palm trees flashing by, occasional houses, thatched shacks; the wind whistling past his ears, and that lithe, powerful body beneath him, with its rippling muscles.

Dee seldom spoke, except an occasional monosyllable that the wind tore away. She rode gracefully and easily, leaning slightly forward to the rush of air.

George called at her occasionally. Where was Azeela? Were they overtaking her and Toroh? Did Azeela know they were following her now?

Dee did not answer. Often she would draw ahead. but a whispered word from George to the brute beneath him, and again the dogs were running side by side.

Presently Dee stopped them; the dogs stood panting, with tongues lolling out.

"What is it?" George demanded. "Where are we?"

George saw that the girl's face was drawn with anxiety.

"Azeela has been trying to find out from Toroh why he takes her to Orleen."

"Yes?" he prompted. "And I wondered—"

"Toroh has told her now. Loto's old plane is there. He wants the plane!"

"Oh!" George's heart sank with dismay. "But the plane is in the Orleen Cavern. How can they get to it? Isn't the cavern guarded?"

"Yes. Wait. Toroh says he can get it. He has a spy there—a man whom we trust. One of the guards."

"Oh!" exclaimed George. "Dee, where are they now?"

"A few miles west of here. I cannot tell how far —Azeela does not know just where we are, either."

"Does Toroh know we're after him?"

"No."

George tried to think coherently. "Can't we overtake them, Dee? Before they reach Orleen?"

"I don't know. Azeela says not. Their dogs are very fast—perhaps faster than ours."

To George came a sudden inspiration. The other plane—the one he and Rogers had come in! It was back in the cavern of Anglese City. He and Dee could get that. He could operate it—he'd have to,

226

now. In it they could fly to Orleen — perhaps by that method get there before Toroh and Azeela.

He explained this swiftly to Dee. "We're not so far from Anglese City, are we?"

"No," she agreed. "It's the best thing to do."

They turned the dogs, starting back over the road they had come.

A new thought occurred to George. "Dee, what does Toroh want with that plane? Is he going to take Azeela north in it?"

The dogs were already at a run, but he caught her answer.

"No. He will take the plane back into time! He wants to get some other greater weapons with which to conquer us!"

CHAPTER XX.

CHILDREN OF THE BAS.

F AHN, Loto and Rogers hurried through the city streets. The faint distant cries of the mob ahead of them drifted back. There were now no Arans to be seen, but the figures of Bas men and women were everywhere, most of them moving in the direction of the palace.

As Fahn and his two companions advanced, the turmoil ahead grew louder. The palace stood on a rise of ground in the midst of a lavish garden, with its swimming pool, its trellised pergolas and its graceful palms. The building was rectangular, of two stories, with huge white columns from the ground to the roof. A broad balcony ran the length of the second story in front. The roof was flat, with palms growing upon it.

A crowd of Bas was surging up the hill toward the palace; in the gardens, the armed mob was already massed, impotently struggling about with

228

vainglorious shouts, but lacking, as yet, the courage to advance upon the building.

Fahn had turned into a side street at the foot of the hill.

"Where are we going?" Rogers demanded. "We've got to get into the palace unseen. How can we?"

"The tower," Loto explained. "There's a secret way in that the Bas do not know."

The tower, which rose like the skeleton of a lighthouse, stood close beside the main palace building, with a covered bridge connecting them at the level of the second floor of the palace.

Swiftly Fahn led the two men to the beach, that lay behind the bluff on which the palace and its tower stood. The moonlit strand was deserted. They come to a thick clump of palmettos in the heavy sand at the foot of the bluff — a green tangled clump higher than a man's head. Into this Fahn unhesitatingly plunged, forcing the fronds aside, pushing his way in with the others after him. Inside the palmetto thicket, a small tunnel mouth leading downward was disclosed.

It seemed an endless journey underground — a black passageway not much higher than their heads and so narrow that they could always touch both its walls with their outstretched arms. The air was heavy and fetid. They went down a slope, then on a level, then up. Once they arrived at an iron grating barring the way. But Fahn opened it in some fashion and it swung on a central, horizontal pivot so that they might crawl under it.

Ahead of them, up the incline, a tiny blue light showed. They reached it, found a small circular staircase and climbed upward into the tower.

The whole process had taken perhaps fifteen minutes. The mob was still in the garden; its shouts and mutterings sounded loud and ominous as the little party ascended the interior of the tower and hastily crossed the covered bridge.

Fahn was still leading. They pushed aside a curtained doorway and found themselves in a broad, second-floor corridor of the palace, dimly lighted. The figure of a white bearded old man was crossing it hastily, disappearing into a room at its further end.

Another room was near at hand, with a latticed

grating in its doorway that now stood open. A soft, blue-white light flooded out through it to the hall. The castle interior was evidently in confusion; cries sounded, mingled with the threatening shouts of the mob outside.

A girl, shaking with fright, stood in the nearer doorway, the light from behind glowing through her soft draperies. Other girls crowded forward from the room — a dozen frightened young girls, no more than matured. They saw Fahn, and ran to him for protection.

"The king's wives," said Loto to his father.

Fahn's face softened; and as the girls huddled round him, he tried to comfort them.

"The guilt within them," muttered Rogers. "They think the Bas are coming to kill them — only them."

Fahn caught the words and his eyes flashed. "There is no guilt here, my friend. They are women born to such as this."

With the girls in a clinging group around him, the scientist proceeded down the hallway, followed by Loto and his father.

The room at the end of the hall — it seemed a sort of audience room — was in confusion. Most of the occupants of the palace were in it. The king was pacing up and down near its entrance — his frightened councillors and advisors around him.

On a low divan sat the queen — a woman of forty — regal in a paneled robe, with her hair dressed high on her head. At her knees two children were huddled — the little prince and princess of the Arans. The queen was bending down over them as the strangers entered. When she saw Fahn with the girl-wives of her king, she frowned, stood up with an imperious gesture and ordered the girls from the room. But Fahn, with a stern command, bade them stay. The queen seemed amazed at the scientist's defiance; the king looked undecided, but he did not interfere.

With Fahn's arrival, the room quieted; its occupants gained confidence. The king seemed utterly relieved. He spoke a few placating words to the queen; but she had withdrawn haughtily to a corner, her eyes flashing at the frightened girls who were huddled across the room.

The mob outside was shouting, surging about, but still lacking courage for a concerted attack. Fahn went to a window, with Rogers and Loto after him. The moonlight outside showed the crowd plainly. The Bas were waving their weapons.

"Look!" exclaimed Loto.

A score or more of men were gathering in a group near the center of the garden. A man mounted the rim of a fountain, inciting them with his shouts. His words had effect. The little knot of men waved their cane-knives and came surging toward the palace entrance. The crowd made way for them, following behind them with shouts of triumph. Missiles were thrown upward at the palace windows; one or two at first, then a hailstorm.

Fahn quietly stepped upon a balcony that ran along the entire front of the building. Loto and his father followed. The moonlight fell full upon them, and the crowd recognized the scientist leader.

A great shout went up — a cry of defiance mingled with fear. The men rushing at the building wavered and stopped; the crowd near at hand began pressing backward.

233

Slowly Fahn advanced to the waist-high parapet; with his hands upon it he stood like an orator facing a friendly throng and calmly waiting for silence. A stone whistled past his head, struck the building and clattered to the stone floor of the balcony; but he did not heed it.

His calmness, the confident power of his demeanor, quieted the mob. In a little open space on the terrace, a leader of the Bas sprang into prominence — a giant man who shouted a brief sentence.

"Mogruud," whispered Loto. "He tells them to listen to what Fahn has to say."

Silence came at last, and then Fahn spoke — quietly, earnestly. He seemed to be winning them, when from the palace behind, the king suddenly appeared on the balcony. At sight of him an angry shout rolled up from the crowd. A long, thin knife, with a tail of feathers on it, flew up from below and stuck quivering in the window casement beside the king's head. The king retreated.

Fahn continued speaking, but now the mob would not listen to him. A woman's shrill laugh of derision floated upward.

234

At once Fahn's tone changed. He rasped out a stern command, but a scattering hail of stones was his answer. Then without warning, his hand went to his robe. He flung a little ball into the air. It burst fifty feet from his hand with a shrill whistling scream, and a shower of sparks scattered downward over the garden. They were harmless, but they sent a mild electric shock through every individual of the mob. The Bas were frightened into silence.

"He does not want to kill even one of them," Loto whispered. "Never before have the Bas been in open demonstration. It might spread to other cities — anything might happen."

Fahn was now whispering into a tiny mouthpiece — talking to his guards at the cavern a mile or so away. From the cavern-mountain across the city a blue-white shaft of light sprang into the sky. The Bas saw it and stared. And then suddenly the air seemed bursting with voices. Four words, repeated by the audible radio that the cavern was sending out.

"*Death to disloyal Bas! Death to disloyal Bas!*"

A million aerial voices were proclaiming it everywhere. And then the words changed.

"*We must win against Toroh! The Bas must help us win against Toroh!*"

The threat and its so swiftly following appeal were irresistible. Mogruud shouted an enthusiastic answer to Fahn; and the crowd applauded.

The voices in the air were presently stilled; the light over the cavern disappeared. And, still with his hands quietly on the parapet, Fahn again addressed the people below him.

"Mogruud says the laws should be changed," Loto whispered swiftly to his father. "The Bas women should have their children without exile."

Fahn seemed to make a sudden decision. He spoke again into his mouthpiece. Again the light sprang over the cavern. From the air came the words:

"*Bas women will not be exiled! Bas children will be free!*"

Surprised, awed, then frantic with joy, the crowd in the palace gardens took up the cry; and all over the island the radio voices were proclaiming it:

"*Bas children will be free! The Scientists promise Bas children will be free!*"

CHAPTER XXI.

A RACE TO THE PLANES.

S TILL side by side, George and Dee rode back toward Anglese City. It was further than George had thought; then he realized that the girl had turned into a different road. He shouted a question at her.

"A shorter way to the cavern," she explained.

The wind whistling past them made conversation difficult. George understood that they were skirting the city to where the cavern stood on its other side. They were still in the open country — a road of white sand, palm lined, with a forest jungle all around, and only an occasional house.

George's mind was in a turmoil. Toroh taking the other plane into time! Memory came to him of all those greater civilizations he and Rogers had seen through the centuries they had passed. Toroh was going back to those civilizations to secure weapons! The thought turned George cold all over. With the weapons from former, greater ages, Toroh and his army of Noths would be invincible.

Words in the wind sweeping by startled George into sudden alertness.

"*Death to disloyal Bas!*"

It seemed as though some tiny voice had whispered it to him.

Dee had checked both the dogs abruptly.

"What's that?" George demanded.

It came again:

"*Death to disloyal Bas! Death to disloyal Bas!*"

The air was whispering it, then calling it — a myriad voices echoed it everywhere.

"Look there!" cried Dee.

Ahead of them, a mile or so away — a blue light was standing up into the sky. There was a house near at hand — a Bas shack. From it a woman and two naked children came running out into the moonlight — panic-stricken at the dread words with which the air resounded.

And then the words changed:

"*Bas women will not be exiled! Bas children will be free!*"

The woman in front of the shack clutched her children, listening, rejoicing — almost unbelieving.

Dee had started the dogs forward again. Swiftly she explained to George what she thought it might mean — a radio proclamation from Fahn. In a few moments the light over the cavern had vanished; the voices in the air died away.

George's mind reverted to their own situation; the incident had given him an idea.

"Dee, where are Azeela and Toroh now?"

She thought an instant; momentarily the mental bond with her sister had been broken.

"Very near Orleen, she thinks. They have heard the voices. Toroh is very angry. He had hoped much that the Bas would rebel. It would have helped him."

"Near Orleen!" George echoed. "Can't we get to the Anglese Cavern first?"

"I think so." She had started Rotan into a run, but George called her to stop. Even at the risk of losing more precious time, he questioned her.

"Dee, listen. Are the Caverns of Orleen and Anglese City connected by radio?"

"Yes," she said.

"Then, listen. We'll get to Anglese City first—tell them to inform the guards at Orleen. When Toroh and Azeela arrive they can seize them—if we warn them ahead."

She nodded with instant comprehension.

"All radio isn't broadcast audibly, is it?" he added.

"No," she said. The dogs were running faster. She called back over her shoulder. "We'll do that. I'll tell Azeela."

They swept forward, the dogs settling low to the ground as they ran. A great weight seemed to have lifted from George. It would be simple enough, after all—merely notify the Cavern of Orleen by radio, and Toroh would be seized when he presented himself with Azeela.

George contemplated the outcome. With Toroh in their hands, the Noth attack would collapse. There would be no war.

It was a race then—the only thing that could go wrong would be if Toroh got to the other cavern first. Rotan and Dee were ahead; the girl's slight figure clinging to the dog showed in the moonlight. George whispered to Atal, thumped the dog's flank with his hand.

As they caught up with Dee, he shouted: "Where's Azeela now? Will we make it?"

"Yes," she answered. "I think so."

The mountain that housed the cavern loomed ahead through the palms; houses lay to the right — the outskirts of Anglese City. Half a mile more and they would be there.

Atal's upflung head brought George out of another reverie. The dog, still running at full speed, was sniffing the air. George heard Rotan growl, and Dee's sharp command for silence.

Another command from the girl, and both dogs stopped; Atal slid on his haunches, checking himself so abruptly that George was flung to the sand.

He was unhurt; he picked himself up to find Dee beside him.

"Some one is coming," she said sharply. "Some one the dogs know is not a friend."

She spoke to the dog, and pulled George to the side of the road where a cluster of banana trees

241

threw an inky shadow. Together they stood there in silence. Atal and Rotan had disappeared. The road was a white ribbon in the moonlight. George listened, but could hear nothing. He tried to question Dee, but she silenced him.

Presently there came the thud of running feet; from the direction of Anglese City two running dogs with riders swept into view. They were men riders — men black cloaked and with masks. Arans, from the festival, George thought.

They would have passed without seeing the lurking figures under the banana trees had not Atal and Rotan, in spite of Dee's command, suddenly charged them from the shadows across the road.

The two men, shouting in anger and alarm, tumbled from their mounts. The four dogs mingled in a snarling, biting mass.

Still George and Dee were unseen in the shadows. One of the men in the road had lost his cloak and mask; the moonlight showed his face.

"One of Toroh's brothers," Dee breathed into George's ear. In the dimness he could see she was raising the small crescent-shaped weapon. Some noise that she or George made must have alarmed the men. They were no more than ten feet away; they looked sharply across the road, and then, evidently seeing nothing, they turned back to where the dogs were still fighting—more silently now, with a deadly fury.

Sparks leaped suddenly from Dee's outstretched hand. The men turned. One of them cried out in terror; but they both stood stiff and motionless.

"We've got 'em!" George shouted. "Good work, Dee!"

He would have leaped forward, but her free hand gripped him.

"George! Quick! The globe!"

One of the men, supposedly stricken beyond the power to move, was by some superhuman effort of will slowly raising his hand; in his fingers the moonlight showed a tiny black globe. It came up, very slowly, as his almost paralyzed muscles struggled with its weight.

But George had recovered his wits. He snatched his own globe from his pocket, pointed it, pulled the trigger.

The night was split by a flash — a tiny, sizzling snap of thunder; the globe recoiled in George's hand. Across the road the bodies of the two men lay motionless on the sand. A sulphurous smell was in the air; and another, gruesome.

Dee was leaning against a banana trunk, panting. Her face had gone white; but she smiled as George turned to her.

"They almost got us," she said.

George himself was trembling, but he would not let her see it.

"Almost, Dee. Next time I'll be ready. I didn't realize —"

Among the trees across the road the dogs were still fighting. One of the Noth dogs lay motionless, torn and bleeding. Atal and Rotan together were attacking the other — the three rolling and tumbling as they bit and tore at each other, their huge bodies trampling down the banana trees as they fought.

"Dee, could I use the thunderbolt on them?"

She shook her head. "Wait."

It lasted only a moment more; the second Noth

dog was down, with Atal's fangs buried in its throat.

The two dogs came leaping back to their mistress, their bodies torn, and matted with dirt and blood.

Dee patted them affectionately, as they stood licking their wounds. "But you should have minded me," she said.

George had taken one look at the two charred figures lying in the road; he drew the girl away.

"Come on. I wouldn't look over there. We must hurry, Dee."

They mounted the dogs and started forward, more slowly this time, for the animals carried them with difficulty.

Again George remembered. Toroh would be at the Orleen Cavern by this time. They had lost! This delay had been the one unexpected thing that could defeat them.

"Dee —"

But the girl had anticipated him.

"They are in the plane." She half whispered the words. "Azeela has been trying to tell me for a long time. Toroh had a spy at the cavern entrance

—a man whom we trust as a Scientist. He let them in — Azeela had no chance to make an outcry. They are in the plane now. Azeela tells Toroh she cannot operate it. Wait! Now he tries the Proton switch himself."

A silence.

"Dee! What is it?" George pleaded.

She shook her head. "Nothing comes. Nothing!"

The connection was broken! Azeela was carried back into time. Had something temporarily stopped her message? Would her thought-bond with her sister hold across the centuries that now separated them?

George could only ask himself these questions with sinking heart. If the bond would not hold, then Azeela was lost to them forever. Lost to Loto, who loved her. And Toroh would get his weapons and win the war — inevitably.

"Nothing yet, Dee?"

"No."

They rode slowly onward. At last Dee gave a cry of joy.

"It comes again! She is all right, George! You hear? All right now." Her voice raised to triumph and thankfulness.

"Oh!" George thumped Atal to urge the dog forward. "Dee, we must hurry. They're going back into time?"

"Yes. Azeela looks at the dials. Twenty-five years back now. She tells us to hurry. She will watch the dials and let me know where they are. Toroh does not suspect anything. He is gloating. He thinks he has won everything."

At last they were ascending the slope to the mouth of the cavern. The yawning hole showed black in the face of the cliff. On the small platform above the mouth a single light disclosed the figures of three guards sitting there.

In the moonlight the guards saw them coming. A bolt of lightning flashed downward across the black hole; a peal of thunder rolled out.

They stopped, and Dee called to the guards. One of them descended from the platform—down a narrow flight of steps cut in the cliff face. He came forward in the moonlight—a black robed figure.

247

Dee spoke with him, and, recognizing a daughter of Fahn, he saluted respectfully. There followed a brief colloquy, then the guard stood aside.

A moment later they were in the cavern. The huge tunnel was dark and dank; but blue-white lights glimmered ahead in the darkness. The place was silent, seemingly deserted.

Down the length of the main tunnel they hurried. The plane stood there in the open space, in the glare of blue-white light. They stood before it.

"Dee, shall we send for your father?"

She hesitated.

"Where is he?" George persisted. "Did you ask the guard?"

"Yes. He and Loto and Loto's father are at the palace. There has been rebellion and murder — the murder of Helene, Mme. Voluptua."

She recounted succinctly the events of the night in Anglese City as the guard had told them to her.

George whistled. "They've got their hands full. Dee, are you still in communication with Azeela?"

"Yes. They are beyond fifty years."

"Going how fast?"

"Azeela says as fast as they can — the twentieth intensity."

George made a decision.

"Dee, we mustn't wait — mustn't stop for anything. You're willing to go?"

"Yes," she declared soberly.

She reached toward the platform. George locked his hands, and she put her small foot into them. He lifted her — she seemed no heavier than a child — and she swung herself up gracefully and easily to the platform.

George followed and closed the cabin door after them. "Did you tell the guard what we were going to do?"

"Yes," she said. "I told him to tell father later to-night — when things were more quiet at the palace."

"Good girl. Dee, have you ever been back into time?"

"No. Azeela has. Just a little way — with Loto. He taught her to operate the other plane."

"Yes. How fast are they going, Dee — the twentieth intensity?"

"Yes."

George's hand was on the Proton switch. He took a last look around.

"Sit down, Dee. Hold the arms of your chair. Don't be frightened."

The cabin was dark; through its windows the blue-white glare outside showed the jagged brown walls of the cavern. The twentieth intensity! Toroh was going as fast as he possibly could!

George pulled the switch. There came a soundless clap in his head; a plunge, headlong into some bottomless abyss; falling for hours — an eternity.

CHAPTER XXII.

GEORGE—OR TOROH?

Fahn's proclamation to the Bas had far-reaching effects. All over the island that night and the next day there was rejoicing. The radio proclaimed a national holiday, which the Bas gave over to festivities.

The murder of Mme. Voluptua was forgotten; the rebellion in Anglese City was a thing of the past. The work of Toroh's spies was completely undone; everywhere they presented themselves now they were seized by the Bas and delivered to the authorities—until by mid-morning none dared show himself. They remained in hiding in the mountains, and the following night fled the island.

Fahn's object had been attained. Everywhere, enthusiasm for the war soon mounted to a patriotic frenzy.

But it was not all smooth sailing for Fahn. Within an hour after the first radio proclamation—just before dawn that day — the king called the Scientist to his audience room and demanded that it be retracted. For the first time within generations, a Scientist defied his king.

Fahn gravely refused. The king, with his councillors — brave now since the mob before the palace had dispersed — clustered around him, vigorously tried to overawe the Scientist. But Fahn was obdurate; respectful to the majesty of royalty — but obdurate nevertheless.

The king was powerless, and he knew it. He raged, threatened, but to no avail.

That afternoon the king's council met. The Scientists were declared outlaws; a call was issued for the Aran police, who were scattered throughout the island, to come at once to Anglese City to defend their sovereign.

It was a monarch struggling against all reason to defend what he considered his birthright. Royalty outraged!

But the Aran police did not come. Worse than that, those near at hand in Anglese City prudently vanished.

252

That same afternoon the Scientists met in Anglese City. Fahn's action was upheld; and from other cities came similar decisions. The government was taken over by the Scientists for the period of the war. Laws ratifying the new status of the Bas women and children were hurriedly passed — and made permanent.

All that day the radio audibly proclaimed events as they transpired. The Arans were not be molested; their relations with the Bas were to proceed as always; and the royal family was to be treated with the outward respect to which its birth and position entitled it.

Three days passed — days that for those in Anglese City were full of activity and anxiety. The Arans kept sullenly to themselves; the king and his councillors shut themselves in the palace; the Bas went about their accustomed tasks — feverishly, abstractedly — waiting for the call to war.

The Scientists, trusting nothing to chance, sought out all the Aran police and disarmed them. All weapons were kept in the caverns, where the manufacturing and assembling went steadily forward.

Fahn, Loto, and Rogers, during these three days, lived at Fahn's home. From George and the two girls, nothing had been heard. They were days full of anxiety — almost despair — for the three men. The guards at the two caverns reported what had happened. Fahn cursed his inefficiency in allowing a Toroh spy to remain unsuspected in the League. The man who had given Toroh the plane was located and put to death — but that helped matters little.

In the brief interims of inactivity the three men discussed what George and Dee might be doing — what the outcome would be. The discussions were futile; there was nothing to do but wait.

The character of the two Frazia planes — the identity of the visitors — had never been made public. Only Fahn and his two companions — and a few of the Scientist leaders — were aware of the momentous outcome for which they were so helplessly waiting.

On the afternoon of the third day, Fahn took Loto and his father through the cavern. Loto was pale and tight-lipped; but he seldom mentioned

254

Azeela, and never once had given vent to his feelings. Rogers was curious to see the cavern; older, more philosophical than Loto, he could throw aside his anxiety over George and the girls. Yet he, too, was more worried than he would have cared to admit, even to himself. The war — the fate of the Anglese — was one thing; but that plane was all that could take him back to Lylda — his wife. He could probably never manufacture another plane in this time world; the materials were not available. He realized now how wrong he had been not to bring Lylda with him.

It was late afternoon when they started. Work in the cavern now proceeded day and night.

To Rogers the place was one of romantic mystery, with a sinister air to it that he could not shake off.

The darkness of the cavern walls, the shadows, the flickering blue lights, and the yawning holes with which the interior of the mountain seemed honeycombed, awed and perturbed him.

Far ahead, down a sharp slope, two blue lights showed. To the left a passageway glowed dull red.

"What's that?" Rogers asked.

255

Fahn turned toward it. They went into the passageway, and from it emerged upon a narrow ledge with a metal railing. Before them spread a huge pit, with the glowing of molten rocks far below — a great pool of lava a thousand feet down — lava that boiled sluggishly, with tiny flames of burning gases licking upward from its surface. To one side, overhead, a rift through the mountain showed a patch of starlit sky.

Visitors to an inferno, they stood clinging to the iron rail. The lurid red light cast monstrous shadows of their figures upward to the rocky ceiling. The sulphurous air was intolerably hot; it choked their breathing. After a moment they all stumbled back into the passageway, coughing, breathing deep of the purer air.

"Fires of the earth so close!" murmured Rogers.

Fahn was leading them forward again. "Yes, almost every mountain on the island is like that. The fires are even closer to the surface at Orleen — we use them in the cavern there."

"And here is a room of medicine and surgery," he added. He had turned them unexpectedly into a side cave—a room furnished and draped, and dimly lighted by braziers hanging from its low roof. Rows of bottles; cases of instruments; a long, low table, littered with a variety of strange objects—the room held a confusion of things, most of which were incomprehensible.

Something made Rogers shudder. "What is that?" he demanded.

"To create human life," said Fahn. "For thousands of years, science has tried to do that. We can make a man's body—but his soul and mind still elude us."

Rogers was staring at a metal framework, where the organs of a man were hanging, joined together, and with a network of blood vessels around them—the fundamental, simplified mechanism of man, without the body. And there was movement to the organs; the heart was beating; the lungs breathing.

It was gruesome; it made Rogers' gorge rise.

"They will function for a little time," said Fahn. "But our surgeons have done better than that. They have made the living body—all but the mind and the soul."

With a dim blue light above it, a small case was standing on a pedestal. A lump of living human flesh lay within—roughly fashioned into human form—arms and legs that kicked.

Rogers backed away.

It seemed a dream, this trip through the Scientists' cavern. From one room to another they wandered. Most of the caves were unoccupied; occasionally a lone worker or a group would stop their tasks momentarily to meet their leader and his visitors.

From far away recesses, where the main work was going on, the hum of dynamos sounded.

"We will not go into the workrooms tonight," Fahn said. "I'll show you them later."

They entered another, inner cave—high-arched and unusually large. It was the museum; it held relics of bygone ages. Broken mechanisms, that the inhabitants of other planets might have left on earth, had been dug up and stored here as in a museum. They meant nothing to Rogers, nor did Fahn offer to explain them. But this room more than any other in the cavern seemed to carry with it the power of science—the greater science that to

Fahn's time world was in the prehistoric past. It showed Fahn and his contemporaries in their true light; they were archaeologists — imitators, reconstructors, not real creators.

At last they reached a circular room equipped with the apparatus for taking voices and images from the air. Its side walls were paneled with huge crystals that mirrored distant scenes; and it was filled with millions of tiny voices.

Fahn stood before one of the crystals; his hand was on a lever; the fingers of his other hand rested on a tiny row of buttons. Rogers noticed that there were scores of similar mechanisms dispersed about the room.

"Let us look and listen, a mile away to the west," Fahn said.

The crystal before them was some six feet square. It was gray and cloudy. Fahn pressed one of the small black buttons, and moved the lever over a notch. The crystal flooded with color. To Rogers it was like looking through a huge window.

"The viewpoint of our station a mile north of here," said Fahn.

"A thirty foot tower," Loto explained. "The lens on it swings in a circle. We are looking westward now — toward Orleen."

The scene in the crystal showed the red western sky; a white road in the foreground, disappearing seemingly at Rogers' feet; the green, palm-dotted island, with twilight shadows creeping upon it; to the left, the island mountain range — peaks rising in serrated ranks, with giant, snow-clad summits.

"It was near here that day before yesterday they found the charred bodies of Toroh's brother and his Noth companion," Loto added. "A Bas woman — see that shack there by the road — she saw a girl and a man passing the night before. It may have been George and Dee."

The shack at the roadside showed plainly. A Bas woman was sitting at its doorway, crooning to her infant. Her voice sounded almost as clearly as though the watchers had been sitting on the small tower where the lens and radio mechanism were perched.

"We will turn," said Fahn.

A panorama unfolding the scene moved slowly

sidewise; the sea to the north, with the mountain range beyond it, dim in the gathering darkness; east, back toward Anglese City, where the cavern-mountain itself showed behind the palms; to the south past a distant vista of the city houses; and still swinging, it came back to the road and the house and stopped — again facing the west.

"Another station," Fahn added.

The crystal-face went dark, and then relighted. It was a viewpoint of a hundred feet in the air this time. Again it swung the points of the compass.

For half an hour Fahn continued his demonstration. There might have been a hundred or more towers scattered over the island; and the scene from any one of them sprang at Fahn's will into the crystal-window.

"What are the other crystal-mirrors for?" Rogers asked Loto.

"The island can be searched by several operators simultaneously. Any viewpoint may be thrown into any crystal; and there are receivers for your ears, so that the sounds you hear will not confuse others in the room."

261

The island was growing dark. The crystal showed a viewpoint from the channel coast halfway to Orleen. It must have been from a very high tower; the sea stretched several hundred feet beneath.

"Those mountains across the water," Rogers remarked, "can't be over twenty or thirty miles from our shores. Is that where Toroh's army will gather?"

"From behind them," said Loto. "To the east —nearer the Atlantic Coast, we think. We—"

Fahn had given a slight exclamation. The room was dark, but the reflected light from the crystal showed the Scientist pointing into the mirrored scene.

"Loto, what is that?"

Above the mountains across the channel, the sky was rose-colored with the fading daylight. A tiny gray shape showed there, silhouetted against the clouds. It was moving. They watched it, breathlessly.

"A Frazia plane!" Rogers murmured.

Like a giant bird it seemed circling. A patch of lighter sky behind showed it more plainly after a moment. It *was* a Frazia plane—unmistakably! It was closer than they had thought—over the channel, but it seemed to be flying north, away from them.

"Which one is it?" Loto whispered. "Father—which one is it?"

But that they could not tell. George, or Toroh? One of them had returned. The plane was flying lower, circling again. The dimness absorbed it; then it reappeared. It seemed now to be flying crazily.

"Out of control!" Loto whispered in horror. "It's falling!"

The plane turned over, fluttered down—was swallowed by the shadows of the distant mountains.

CHAPTER XXIII.

THE PURSUIT THROUGH TIME.

THE interior of the plane was glowing. The familiar humming sounded. George and Dee had started back into time.

"Dee! Dee! You all right?"

Her wan smile reassured him. "Where are we?"

"Going back into time," he said cheerfully. The dials were beside him. "Nearly forty years from where we started already. You'll feel all right soon."

"I am all right," she persisted. "I mean, George, are we still in the cavern?"

The question brought an idea to George that made his heart race. They *were* still in the cavern, at a time forty years previous. What was the cavern like then? Suppose its entrance was closed! How could they get out?

Through the windows nothing could be seen but blackness. George hesitated.

"Dee, can your thoughts still reach Azeela?"

"Yes," she said. "She was frightened for me. She knows now we are coming after her. She and Toroh are past one hundred years."

"Still going?"

"Yes."

"Where are they in space?"

"She says in the air, over the Orleen Cavern. She thought it best to show Toroh how to fly the plane —she was afraid to remain underground."

"So am I," said George. "But we're here—we'd better get out."

There were headlights on the plane; their glare showed the tunnel. George started up the Frazia motors, slowly; they rolled forward, faster as they left the tunnel-mouth and took the air.

The scene was that familiar grayness—new to Dee. Beneath them lay the island—the blurred, gray city to one side.

"Over Orleen," George mused. "We must get there quickly. Further back in time the city will not be there—we might get lost in space."

At an altitude of perhaps a thousand feet they flew swiftly westward. Orleen was there when they reached its space; the dials were beyond two hundred years.

"Azeela is here," Dee announced. "She says the city is dwindling."

"What do her dials say? Will Toroh let her look at them?"

"Yes. She is very careful. He suspects nothing. She says the dials are nearly two hundred and thirty years."

"We're catching them," George exclaimed triumphantly. "We've got the faster plane. We'll catch up with them. Where are they exactly? In space I mean."

A brief pause.

"Azeela says almost directly over the peak near the east edge of the city — the cavern peak."

There were twin peaks, not over six hundred feet apart. The cavern peak was the northern one; through the floor window now, George could see the summit of the other, directly beneath his plane.

"How high is Toroh? They're using the helicopters?"

"Yes."

"How high up?"

"She says about five hundred feet."

It was the altitude at which George and Dee were hovering. George gazed through the side window. The other peak showed plainly. Above it was the exact space Toroh and Azeela were occupying. Their plane was invisible, of course—twenty-five years into the past.

Dee sat silent, communicating with her sister; and George fell into a reverie. What a wonderful thing thought was! Of everything, only thought could roam the universe at will—could bridge the gap across the years without regard to time and space.

"They've passed three hundred years, George," the girl's voice aroused him. "Three hundred years just now."

"Two hundred and ninety," he read from their own dials. "Only ten years away! We'll overtake them presently."

In the stress through which they had passed, and their excitement, neither of them had considered what they would do when they overtook Toroh.

Indeed, it was Azeela who brought it to their minds with her anxious questions to Dee.

George did not know what they would do; nor did Dee. It had seemed necessary first to overtake Toroh; and to accomplish that had occupied their entire attention.

They stared at each other in dismay.

"How about my thunderbolt globe?" George suggested.

"We cannot use it," she reminded. "If we destroy the other plane, Azeela would be killed."

It was obvious. They could not attack the other plane under any circumstances. But Toroh was going to stop for weapons. They would have to stay near him, both in space and time; and when he stopped, and perhaps left the plane, they would rush up and rescue Azeela.

It was all either of them could plan.

"Keep as near them as we can," said George. "That's the idea. And watch our chance. Tell Azeela to keep you posted on everything."

They slowed their time-flight a trifle; it would have been foolish to let Toroh see them — merely put him on his guard. At a distance of about ten years they followed.

At eight hundred years before the events they had left the city of Orleen had disappeared. The island looked almost the same; the peaks were still there. But now among the palms there seemed only a few rude shacks — the earliest Bas settlers.

The time-velocity of both planes was steadily increasing. Azeela's messages told them that the other plane was still hovering motionless. There was nothing to do. They waited, anxiously at first, and then, after an interval, fell into earnest conversation.

"Suppose we can't rescue Azeela," George suggested once. "Toroh will use her as a hostage against your father, won't he? Offer her life, perhaps, if your father will help him in the war?"

She nodded soberly.

"That's why he abducted her before, Loto said. Did he make the offer then?"

"No. But he was going to."

"Why didn't you go after her?" he suggested. "Didn't she send back messages to you, Dee?"

"Yes. But he took her north into the snow. She did not know where she was. Father sent out an expedition. They couldn't find her. The Noths attacked them. They came back, and they were going to start again when Loto returned her to us."

"Oh," said George. He thought a moment. "I wonder what your father would have done — what he would do now if Toroh holds Azeela and offers her life against the war. Would your father let Toroh kill her?"

She hesitated. "I think he would," she said at last. "It would be a nation against one life. He would sacrifice himself, I know. And I think he would even sacrifice Azeela."

George met her earnest dark eyes — so sparkling, usually, but now so somber.

"Would you, Dee?"

"No," she said impulsively.

"Neither would I," he declared. "I wouldn't let harm come to Azeela for all the Anglese — or harm to — to you, either."

She did not answer. Presently he said:

"I was thinking about that Aran Festival, Dee.

You know you oughtn't to go to affairs like that. *Do* you know it?"

Her gaze met his again, questioningly. "It is part of life," she said. "My father thinks Azeela and I should know what life is. In your time-world was it wrong?"

George felt himself flushing. "Wrong? What, the festival?"

"No. That is evil—much of it is wrong, and foolish as well as evil. I mean my going there—a girl of the Scientists, who is not like the Aran women?"

"Yes," said George stoutly. "I—I didn't want you to be there." His hand impulsively touched hers. "I didn't like it, Dee. You're too nice a girl. And I don't think Loto liked Azeela being there, either."

Instead of answering, she gave a sudden cry.

"What is it?" George demanded in alarm.

She had no opportunity to reply. Through the side window the other plane showed less than a thousand feet away—a shimmering ghost that was gone as soon as they had seen it!

George leaped to the Proton switch, but Dee checked him.

"Wait! Wait till Azeela tells what happened."

In the absorption of their conversation, Azeela's messages had been ignored. Toroh had slackened his time-flight; he was preparing to land. It was an unfortunate occurrence, for Toroh had seen the other plane. He still did not guess that Azeela herself was guiding the pursuit.

Again, without warning, the other plane showed. This time it was flying — coming directly toward them. George held his breath. Toroh's plane was so close he had no opportunity even to move from his seat. It was running level with them in time; it was charging them! Had Toroh gone mad? He would kill them all!

It was no more than a second or two. Through the window George caught a brief glimpse of the shimmering thing rushing at them. Then it swerved upward.

"He's going to fire a thunderbolt!" Dee gasped.

George was aware of a flash; but he had not seen it, only imagined it.

The attacking plane swept overhead and vanished —dissolved into nothingness!

Toroh had fired a thunderbolt. The rush of electrons traveling at the speed of light from Toroh's plane to George's had been too slow. The mark was gone into a different time before the thunderbolt could reach it!

The incident left George and Dee shuddering; but confident now, that so long as they kept moving through time, Toroh could not harm them.

George's dials now registered the passage of some sixty-eight hundred years. He was amazed. Then he realized how long he and his companion had been talking; and the time-velocity at the twentieth intensity had been accelerating tremendously. He had forgotten to look beneath him; he did so now, and the island was not there! The channel was gone; the mountain range had disappeared. The cataclysm that had formed the island had been passed.

Azeela's messages told that her plane was now nearly a hundred years nearer the Anglese time-world. Toroh, finding his attack ineffective, had given it up. He had started a horizontal flight; he was looking for a city in which he could land.

George and Dee sat helpless, for Azeela could not describe which way she was flying.

"Lost!" George exclaimed. "We've lost them! Of course, she can't tell us which way they're going when there's nothing down there but gray forests — and blurred gray sky overhead."

It seemed probable that they would never see Toroh's plane again. Already it was many miles from them in space — in what direction they could not guess.

Back through time the two planes swept, invisible to each other, yet no more than a few hundred years apart. The rescue of Azeela — for the present at least — was certainly impossible. Toroh was looking for a civilization — some gigantic city — where he might secure weapons. George decided he must do the same. With Dee he discussed it earnestly, and again, temporarily, Azeela's thought-messages were ignored.

At fifteen thousand years — more than halfway back to the time-world of the New York City of

George's birth — structures began rising out of the forests. By retrograded changes made visible, at first they seemed moldering ruins, then, broken, neglected areas of deserted cities; then the inhabited cities themselves.

At eighteen thousand years George and Dee were poised no more than a few miles from where Orleen stood so many centuries later. A huge river with a delta emptied into the open gulf; a broad expanse of lake was near by. And on both sides of the river and around the lake a gigantic city rose in terraced buildings of masonry and steel. Dee stared in awe at its towers, bridges, aerial streets with the monorail structures stretching above.

"We might land here," George suggested. "Shall we, Dee? You'd think they'd have something to help your father in the Anglese war."

She nodded; and he prepared to land on an open space a few miles north of the city outskirts. They came to the ground — at the third intensity of Proton current. Everything was gray — soundless.

"All ready, Dee?"

"Yes."

He flung over the switch. When the shock of stopping had passed, George stood up; Dee was already on her feet beside him.

It was night outside; lights were flashing. They rushed to the window. The sky was lurid with bursting colored bombs; an inferno of noise sounded — shrill electrical screams; an intermittent pounding that seemed to shake the earth.

From almost overhead a red rocket exploded. Its light persisted — illumined with a vivid red glare the scene for miles around. The giant city buildings were visible. As George stared, a great flame seemed to leap from the sky. One of the buildings fell.

Nearer at hand a cloud of swarming mechanisms came out of the air — swooping down — circling. Beams of light from them and from the city crossed like swords in the sky. The earth under the plane was rocking. Beside it a green flash struck and sent rocks, bowlders, and dirt up like a waterspout.

"George! George!"

Dee's terrified cry at his ear was almost drowned by the scream of dynamos — the whistling, bursting, and pounding.

George's trembling fingers found the Proton switch. He pulled it. The inferno of the night melted, slipped away into a gray, soundless blur.

War! They had fallen into the midst of a battle —that giant earth-city defending itself, perhaps against invaders from another planet.

"We won't try that again," George murmured.

"Azeela," said the girl suddenly. "She tells me that Toroh has secured weapons! He is returning to our time-world!"

Toroh had landed at another city, in another time, but still in that same greater civilization. He had chosen a night—had bound Azeela—left her in the plane—had stolen weapons the use of which he could learn by experimenting.

George listened blankly. "What sort of weapons?"

"Azeela does not know. One large piece of apparatus. He has it in the plane—covered by a black bag. He will not let her touch it. And there are other things—a pile of disks or something. White—like steel. She cannot see them well—he has covered them also. Many small disks, she

277

thinks. He is triumphant. His plane is going to-ward Anglese City — fast."

"In space or time?"

"In time. In space they are hovering. Azeela does not know where they are. Toroh says he will wait. When the time-world of the island is reached they will recognize the land. Then Toroh will take Azeela among the Noths. He says if our father does not yield he will kill her. And then he and the Noths will conquer the Anglese."

George had lost. He confessed it to Dee — but still there seemed nothing that they could do but try and keep as close to the other plane in time as they could.

Toroh's plane was sweeping forward. He had released Azeela, commanding her to instruct him more in detail in the handling of the Frazia motors. Azeela's dials now read some fifty-five hundred years behind the Anglese time-world. George's simultaneously read about six thousand.

They came to the cataclysm that formed the island. George had forgotten it, but he chanced to be gazing down. The gray forests suddenly blurred — vague chaos possessed the earth, the air, and the sky; then there were the familiar mountains, the channel, the island! A myriad details of those hours of upheaval had been compressed, blended into a fraction of a second. The eye and the mind could not grasp it. The thing was past, done and away — with only its *effect* left as evidence that it had occurred.

George and Dee were above the channel and west of Orleen. No more than a hundred years now separated the planes.

"What shall we do?" George demanded for the tenth time. And then an idea came to him. They could not attack Toroh until he reached his destination. He would be among his own army then; a rescue of Azeela would be impossible. But now, if Azeela could separate herself from Toroh, he could never find her in time and probably wouldn't try.

George explained it to Dee. Azeela was not bound; could she persuade Toroh on some pretext to land on the ground — and then leap from the plane? The shock of stopping in time should be no different than when the plane itself stopped.

Azeela had already thought of it; the idea had been prompted by the fact that Toroh's plane was running out of petrol. He would have to conserve it — not use it with the helicopters, or else he would have none left with which to get up north.

George was trembling with excitement. "Tell her to suggest that they land."

Toroh was at that instant landing. It was a familiar spot to Azeela; she described it exactly to Dee, and the younger sister recognized it.

Toroh's plane had entered the second century before Fahn's time-world when George — some fifty years further back — arrived at the spot in space Azeela was describing. There was the little rise of ground, with the channel beyond. The vegetation was different, but the level rock was there. And on the level rock Azeela said that Toroh's plane was resting.

Dee's voice was shaking so that she could hardly talk. "Will it — kill her, George?"

He was white faced, tense — but he shook his head.

"Tell her to read the dials as exactly as she can."

280

Azeela read them. George held his watch in his hand; he noted the hour and minute it gave.

"She has called Toroh's attention to something outside," Dee's voice translated swiftly. "She opens the cabin door. He is behind her — but he does not suspect."

George kept his eyes on his watch. Two minutes since Azeela gave them her dial-reading; and he knew the approximate time-velocity of the other plane.

Three minutes!

"She is on the platform. The blurred rock is only a few feet below her. Azeela pretends something is wrong under the plane. Toroh is beside her — but he does not touch her. He does not suspect she would dare — "

Three minutes and a half.

"She jumps — "

George waited. "Is she all right? Is she all right?"

Silence.

"Can't you get her? Oh, Dee, can't you get her?"

The communication was broken.

CHAPTER XXIV.

THE FLYING LENS.

"IT fell," Rogers murmured. "Was that Toroh's plane — or George's?"

Loto did not answer; he stared with set face at the crystal mirror which was turning purple with the deepening shadows of nightfall. The mountains into which the plane had fallen were a vague silhouette against a sky of stars.

"If we could only see over there," Rogers added wistfully. "Is this tower we're looking from now the nearest to the mountains, Loto?"

It was the nearest. But Fahn was talking swiftly into a small mouthpiece beside him.

"We may be able to see into the mountains," he said in a moment. "We must find out which plane it was. Perhaps Toroh fell and was killed."

The anxiety on his face belied the calmness of his tone; his two daughters were out there; possibly one or both had met death in that falling plane.

A man entered the cave-room hurriedly — a solitary worker whom Fahn had summoned from another part of the cavern — a youngish man with spectacles of darkened glass; he was black-robed; and gloved.

Fahn questioned him briefly; he brightened; nodded, and hastened away again.

Loto explained: "He's been working on a new invention, father. We hoped to use it in the war — but now we fear the attack may come before it is ready. There is only one small model constructed — finished today."

The man returned with a small mechanism — a black circular disk, an inch thick and two feet in diameter. On it was mounted a cone-shaped lens a foot high. It did not look unlike a tiny model of the lens of a lighthouse. Beside the lens an operating mechanism was fastened — an open box in which tiny coils of wire showed. And near this was what looked like a miniature searchlight.

Fahn inspected the apparatus. His assistant made some connections, adjusting another mechanism on the table. Then, turning the disk over and holding it in the air above his head, he released it. The thing floated motionless; its lens-tower was hanging downward; the small searchlight pointed downward; from it a beam of blue-white light struck the cave-floor with a circle of brilliant illumination.

Fahn smiled his approval; the young assistant seemed gratified.

"A development of the radio towers, combined with the radio dais you saw at the Festival — the apparatus Toroh's brothers tried to steal," Loto said to his father.

A moment later the young scientist had disappeared with his flying lens — taken it outside the cavern to release it into the air.

Fahn sat at the table, with the newly installed mechanism under his fingers. In a few moments the assistant was back, empty-handed; he stood before the now blank crystal mirror with the other men, anxiously watching for the success of his work.

"This was greatly used a few centuries ago," Fahn said. He sighed. "Our ancestors knew so much; it is so hard to keep up with them."

The crystal mirror presently became illumined.

The scene was the darkness of night — stars reflected moonlight from a moon just outside the line of vision. Below — a thousand feet perhaps — a vague palm-dotted landscape was sliding.

To the watchers, the illusion was like flying through the night, and looking downward.

"I shall light the searchlights," Fahn said.

A broad circle of blue-white illumination fell upon the shifting land beneath. Across it, the palms of the island were moving backward. The viewpoint of the whole scene was unsteady. The horizon came up and down, like the horizon viewed from a plunging ship. The moon showed momentarily — then swung sidewise out of sight.

Soon the channel was beneath; the dark mountains were coming nearer; they tilted downward, almost out of sight, as the lens mounted an incline to pass above them.

"Can we find where the plane fell?" Loto asked anxiously.

Fahn did not answer at once. At last he said: "It will be difficult. It may have fallen behind the mountains; or into them. I do not know."

In the mirror the shifting viewpoint presently showed the mountains from above; the searchlight circle was sweeping across a tumbled land of crags, plateaus and ravines—a white land of snow lying thick on the higher peaks. The lens were circling now; the turning, swaying viewpoint made the watchers dizzy.

At last they saw it—a broken plane lying on its crumbled wing. The searchlight clung to it; the lens lowered, until in the mirror the image of the plane seemed more than a hundred feet below.

"Toroh's plane!" Rogers exclaimed.

There were figures about the plane—moving figures, men and dogs. The men were dragging some apparatus from it—loading it onto a sled. One of the men was Toroh! The viewpoint was close enough now to distinguish him—alive!

But the flying lens had descended too close; the Noths were staring upward. A flash mounted from below; the crystal mirror turned almost a blinding white—then went black.

A thunderbolt from Toroh had struck the flying lens and destroyed it.

CHAPTER XXV.

REUNION.

GEORGE and Dee gazed from their hovering plane at the empty surface of the level rock face below them. Somewhere in time — Azeela was lying there — unconscious, killed perhaps, for the thought messages from her were stilled. Had Toroh gone on? Or had he stopped to try and find her?

They were anxious moments for George and Dee — moments that by George's watch stretched into an hour or more. They were both at the point of exhaustion. They had eaten a little — the plane was provisioned — but they had not slept throughout the trip. George made a close calculation; he knew the time-speed of Toroh's plane; he could estimate closely what Toroh's dials must have read at the instant Azeela jumped.

They found her at last, lying on the rock unconscious. They stopped, carried her into the plane, and before they started again they had revived her. There was a heart stimulant among the plane's medicines; she drank it gratefully. She was not injured, though badly bruised by her fall. She had been knocked unconscious as she left the plane. The instant her body parted contact with its vibrations, blackness had come to her; she did not remember striking the rock.

George was jubilant. Had he been able to rest, he would have wanted to go on after Toroh. But he did not dare rest.

"We'll go on home," he said. "You're a brave girl, Azeela." He smiled down at her as she lay stretched on the leather seat. "I'll start slowly; you've had all the shock you can stand."

That same night in which the flying lens had been destroyed found George piloting his plane into the cavern at Anglese City. Fahn and Rogers were there to greet it. George handed down the girls, and descended with a flourish. In the excitement of his triumphant return he forgot how tired and sleepy he was.

Loto at the moment was in another part of the

cavern. He came hastening forward. He did not see Azeela at first.

"George!"

"Hello, Loto! Here we are. Were you worried?"

Then Loto saw Azeela.

"I brought her back to you," George said softly. "There she is, old man — all safe and sound."

But Loto did not hear him; his arms were around Azeela.

George turned to Dee. "You think he'd sacrifice her for the whole nation of the Anglese? I should say not!"

CHAPTER XXVI.

DEPARTURE FOR BATTLE.

A MONTH went by — days and weeks of activity throughout the island. To the Scientists it was a time of unparalleled stress and anxiety. The government was in their hands for the first time in history, and a war — the first that any individual of that time-world had ever faced — was impending.

With Toroh's return his attack would not long be postponed. Fahn knew it. The radio proclaimed it to the Bas everywhere. An army must be trained at once; the Bas, Arans and Scientists were appealed to for volunteers.

It was Fahn's plan not to wait for the Noths to land on the island; but to anticipate the attack and send an army to meet it. The nation responded to the appeal. Conscription had been considered, but within a day the Bas had offered themselves in such numbers that it was obvious any form of conscription would be unnecessary.

The second day after the radio appeal for volunteers the fact became evident that the Arans were refusing to go to war. In every village recruiting stations were listing the names of the young men of the Bas who presented themselves; and no Arans came. By the audible broadcasting Fahn called them severely to account; but still they remained away, or in hiding. They were sought out. Cowardice, sullenness, declaration that their birthright made it unnecessary — they seemed to have a score of reasons, but the fact remained they would not willingly serve.

Scenes of violence were reported the next day. A Bas father, giving two sons to the coming war, had struck down an Aran youth whom he encountered; a party of Bas, angered into unlawfulness, had entered an Aran household in Orleen, beaten an Aran gathering who were holding festivities; an Aran woman had been killed.

"Serves them right," George exclaimed indignantly. "I'd kill them all."

Fahn was perturbed; then he shrugged. "We have far more young men from the Bas than we can use. I shall tell them to ignore the Arans. And in warfare such as this an unwilling fighter is worse than none."

"Damned cowards," George muttered. "We'll save their hides for 'em, while they stay home and have parties."

The Scientist had caught the words. "Yes, George. Because now that is easiest for us. I want no trouble here on the island. But afterward — when we have won — then we can deal with the Arans."

"I wouldn't have 'em on the island," George declared; and he would have been an unfortunate Aran youth who had encountered George during the days that followed.

The recruiting — hand in hand with the manufacturing activities of the cavern — went steadily on. In every principal village the Bas youths were registered, and drilled, as yet without weapons, officered by older men of the Bas, waiting for the equipment and orders to come to them from Anglese City.

The information Fahn held regarding Toroh and his Noth army was vague, unsatisfactory; and its very meagerness seemed to forecast disaster. Somewhere beyond the mountains the Noths were gathering along the Atlantic Coast. Men and fighting dogs in hordes were coming southward. But their scientific equipment of weapons was practically unknown. The thunderbolt globes — of what power Fahn could not say — were all that he was positive they possessed.

It was Toroh's trip back into time that seemed to hold the greatest menace. He had secured some apparatus. What was it? Something invincible, perhaps — something so completely different from anything with which the Anglese were familiar that they could not hope to cope with it.

There were no answers to these questions.

The flying lens — the only one the Anglese possessed — had been destroyed. Others were now being hastily constructed. With them Fahn intended to reconnoiter extensively over the Noth territory. The information thus attained would be immensely valuable.

The principle of this radio-controlled flying platform, as Fahn had said, was newly invented. It was not yet wholly practical. The dais at the Festival was the first crude model; the flying lens was the second. It had been so successful a model for a beginning that Fahn was encouraged to use it with a broader scope. Larger platforms were now being built. On them thunderbolt projectors were to be mounted — projectors with an effective radius of a thousand feet. A number of these flying platforms would constitute a mechanical army. Controlled by radio whose operators stayed safely at home, it could be sent forth to battle — with the human army to follow behind it.

The perfecting of the electric fabric repulsive to the earth — an invention revived out of the past and brought to practicability only within the last few months — was the basis of the equipment for the Anglese army now being mobilized. It was kept secret until the last moment.

Two weeks after George's return the first flying organization was equipped. Two hundred young men selected from the ranks of the Scientists began drilling secretly at night in an open space near Anglese City. Among them were George and Loto.

To George the experience was the most extraordinary he had ever undergone. The fabric was like thin black gauze. A loose suit of it incased him, bound tightly at his wrists, throat and ankles. About his waist was strapped a broad cloth belt with several pockets in which he would carry various weapons. There was some sort of a battery attached to the belt, from which a current was turned into the gauze suit.

Adjustments of the current to George's normal weight were made by one of Fahn's assistants, while George stood eying the man fearsomely. He could feel the current as it was turned on. It was not unpleasant; it made him tingle all over.

In another moment George was ready. Thin cloth slippers were on his feet; by the pressure against the soles he felt as though he weighed not more than five pounds. Involuntarily he clutched at Loto, who stood beside him. He felt that a breath of wind would blow him away.

"Let go," Loto grinned. "Make a leap, George."

Obediently George leaped gingerly into the air. He floated upward, turned over, arms and legs flying, and floated downward, landing gently on his face in the sand. But after a few trials he could hold his balance; the air seemed fluid, like water. With wings fastened to his arms and legs, he could have swum through it.

He suggested that to Loto. Why, with practice, a man could swim through the air, darting about like a fish through water.

Loto laughed. "You'd make an inventor, George. That probably was the first crude way it was used. But later they developed a much better way of propulsion, and we have revived it now."

The motive power consisted of a single metal cylinder to be held in the left hand — an apparatus which in weight and shape was not unlike an ordinary hand flash light. As George understood its fundamental principle, the thing altered the density of the air in whatever direction it was pointed.

Loto tried to explain it with as few technical words as he could. A spreading, invisible ray from the cylinder penetrated the air for a distance of some ten feet. It separated the molecules of the air, drove them apart. Its action was incredibly swift.

"Well," demanded George.

"The atmosphere exerts a pressure here now of some sixteen pounds to the square inch," said Loto. "The air immediately in advance of this cylinder mouth is almost instantly thinned out. The ray charges the molecules of air — makes them slightly repellent. The result is, George, that immediately in advance of your body the atmospheric pressure is somewhat lessened. Thus, your body moves forward, pushed by the air pressure from behind."

The cylinder had a sliding lever by which its ray was turned on or off. George held it over his head and moved the lever. His body left the ground — shot straight up at increasing speed. There was no rush of wind toward him; instead the air from below seemed to be wafting him upward.

The ground was dropping away. Fifty feet! A hundred feet! Panic struck George; all he could think of to do was shut off the cylinder power. At once he floated down, turning over helplessly. He landed quite gently, several hundred feet from where he had started, with Loto running there to meet him, laughing at his discomfiture.

You couldn't very well get hurt, that was the beauty of the thing. George plunged with enthusiasm into learning how to handle himself in the air.

With a week this organization of two hundred Scientist young men were fairly expert with the new flying apparatus. There were several thousand Bas youths now registered in different parts of the island; but the suits and air cylinders for them were not ready. Finally, another hundred were released; and at Anglese City, Mogruud, the Bas leader, and a hundred selected Bas young men began learning to use them.

In spite of the indignant protests of Loto and George, both Fahn's daughters urged that they be allowed to try the apparatus; and Fahn gave his permission.

"I have no sons to give," he said quietly. "And this warfare is of skill, not strength or endurance. If my girls can help their country, it is their duty — and mine to make the sacrifice."

With this precedent, other Scientist girls — several at Orleen, and twenty at Anglese City — enthusiastically volunteered. Without exception, the girls proved superior to the men. The new art demanded a deft agility—a quickness of thought and movement—a lack of giddiness—which to the girls seemed to come more naturally.

Within a few days Azeela and Dee could dart through the air with incredible dexterity. The cylinder held in the left hand could be pointed quickly in any direction and the body would be drawn that way. Dee especially became proficient. She could dart upward, turn, come swooping down head-first or with slow somersaults, graceful as a diving girl, to right herself a few feet above the ground and land on tiptoe.

The result of the girls' proficiency was that they were organized into a separate squad. There were twenty-eight girls in all; thirteen commanded by Azeela, and thirteen by Dee.

During all this time, the Arans had remained in seclusion, keeping off the streets as much as possible. The Bas, drilling without weapons, were eager to be equipped. The king and his council confined themselves to the palace at Anglese City.

There were no boats, except crude sailing canoes,

on the island. A few of the newly equipped flying corps went northward; but Fahn, anticipating the completion of other flying lenses, ordered them not to cross the channel. In the cavern, day and night, operators watched the mirrors, flashing the viewpoints from every coast tower on the island, to guard against a surprise attack.

A month had passed since George's return in the plane. He had suggested several times that the plane might be used in the war. But Rogers refused this. George had exhausted the Proton current to the point where now there was barely enough left for a return to Rogers's time-world. And the plane in itself, as a means of flying through space, would have been of little value in this warfare.

The flying discs, mounted with observing lenses, and with thunderbolt projectors, were now ready. They were sent out one night, controlled from the cavern.

It was the first aggressive act of the war — a mechanical army of a hundred thunderbolt globes sweeping northward to attack the enemy.

In the cavern room, Fahn and his friends sat

watching the mirrors, which showed the scene from the viewpoint of the flying mechanisms.

The discs swept northward, following the coastline. Beyond the mountains, far ahead, loomed a great encampment close to the shore, dim and vague in the moonlight. In a few minutes the mechanisms would be there.

Suddenly, one of the mirrors in operation went black. In the others, the scene showed that Toroh was sending up some opposing mechanisms. Dots of silver were mounting from the encampment. They floated slowly upward, but they seemed to seek out the Anglese flying platforms — pursuing them as though with human intelligence.

One by one the mirrors were going black, as the flying lenses were being destroyed. In a moment only one was left. It was almost over Toroh's encampment — almost in range where it could have discharged its bolt.

In the mirrored scene, a white dot was growing as it came closer to the lens. Its image grew; it resolved itself from a dot, so what Fahn saw was a thin, gleaming disc. It looked as though it might be whirling. The thing turned, pursued the lens — overtook it — the last mirror went dark.

The operators left their instruments and gathered around Fahn in perturbation. Toroh had sent up some unknown mechanisms; the flying thunderbolt platforms had crashed to the ground before any of them had come within range of the enemy.

It was during this same night that Toroh first used his broadcasting radio. Fahn's radio voices in the air had constantly been encouraging his people. Now, abruptly, the air burst forth with other voices. Somewhere in the mountains across the channel, Toroh had erected a broadcasting station. He was sending threats through the air to the Anglese!

It was a surprise; and it disturbed Fahn greatly: Everywhere on the island aerial voices of the enemy were leering, threatening, boasting of the coming triumph of the Noths. Would the Bas be intimidated? It might be disastrous; for, with the defeat of the flying discs, more than ever now Fahn was depending upon the Bas army.

All that night and the next day, the radio from the cavern sent forth its cheering messages.

By the following noon information began coming to Anglese City that the Bas were apparently not alarmed. They were jeering back at Toroh's aerial voices; but they were demanding vigorously that the Scientists give them weapons.

"In a week we shall be ready," Fahn told Rogers. "Five thousand air-pressure cylinders we have now at the last process of manufacture. The other weapons are ready. One week more is all we need."

Amid Toroh's aerial threats that day had come the reiterated triumphant statement that in two weeks more his attack would come. Two weeks still! It was more than Fahn had hoped for.

The statement was Toroh's trickery. Eighteen hours later — the next morning at dawn — a member of the aerial patrol over the channel returned hurriedly to Anglese City with the news that Toroh's expedition had started by water. Huge barges were coming down the coast, pulled by the giant dogs swimming before them — barges crowded with men and dogs and apparatus.

That morning was one almost of chaos. The invaders would enter the channel near Anglese City.

The thunderbolt projectors which had been distributed thinly about the coast were rushed eastward and concentrated at the channel-mouth. There was no time now to equip the main Bas army. The attack would have to be repelled by the coast defense, and by the small aerial army already formed — one hundred Bas led by Mogruud, two hundred Scientists with whom Loto and George were to serve; and the twenty-six Scientist girls, led by Azeela and Dee.

The radio that morning ordered every able-bodied Bas man on the island to come toward Anglese City with every dog that could be procured. If the invaders landed, the dogs could best oppose them.

It was at this juncture that the king announced the change of his royal capital to Orleen. The royal family, the councillors, their retainers — all fled in their dog carriages from Anglese City. Orleen, much further down the channel, would be safe. News of the king's action spread over the island. Arans from everywhere fled after him, huddling in Orleen.

In the confusion of those hours, the contempt for the Arans passed almost without comment. Orleen was the safest place, and the Bas there — men and women both — scorning to remain among the cowards — came eastward.

By noon the flying army was fully accoutered and ready — in a field near Anglese City. Loto, equipped to remain in constant telephonic communication with Fahn, was virtually its leader. George, with his several weapons in his belt, stood beside Loto. Mogruud had his hundred Bas around him. The girls were in two small groups apart.

At a signal from Fahn, the little army rose swiftly into the sunlit sky. The watching throng was stricken silent with awe. The figures in the air arranged themselves in a broad arc, with the officers tiny specks in front; and then swept forward, over the channel toward the mountains and the distant sea.

CHAPTER XXVII.

THE BATTLE IN THE CHANNEL.

THE palm-dotted island fell silently away. Ahead lay the blue channel; to the right the open sea. To George the flight — the first of any duration he had taken — was exhilarating. It was soundless; the absence of any rush of air against him made it totally unlike flying in a plane. He seemed to be wafting forward as though the air were his native element.

Loto was just ahead of him. Behind him came the army, maintaining its arc-like formation. A little in front, and at a slightly lower level, were the two squads of girls. They were all slim, graceful creatures, most of them under twenty. The black gauze — loose trousers and blouse — showed the white of their limbs beneath. Their heads were bound in deep-red rubber cloth, tight over the forehead and tied in back with flowing ends. With cylinders extended from the left hand they slid forward through the air head-first, in attitudes as

306

though plunging gracefully in a horizontal dive through water.

Though George felt no rush of air, he found he could not talk to Loto, even though no more than twenty feet separated them. The rushing wind between them tore away the words.

Soon they were over the channel. The girls were drifting much lower now. George saw Loto dart down a few feet; then as though he had changed his mind, he came up again. George saw him reach for a mouthpiece that dangled under his chin. He fitted it to his mouth. His voice, magnified to a stentorian roar, rolled out.

"Azeela! Dee! Come higher! You must not go so low!"

Obediently the two girls rose to the higher level, their little squads following them. When they were over the mouth of the channel, George saw Toroh's barges — tiny dark smudges on the water some miles up the coast and a mile or so off shore. His heart leaped, began pounding in spite of his efforts to quiet it.

Following Loto he swept diagonally upward and

forward. Presently he saw that there were six of the barges. They were tremendous things, crowded with men and dogs and mechanical apparatus. Spread over each was a huge caging of flashing silver metal. One barge was some distance in the lead; the others straggled out irregularly behind it for perhaps a mile. All the Noth vessels were being drawn slowly through the water by ranks of harnessed dogs swimming before them.

Loto momentarily had shut off his cylinder; his speed was slackening. George overtook him, put an arm on his shoulder. The nearest of the barges was now less than a mile ahead.

A flash upward from the leading barge was followed in a few seconds by a crack of thunder. The bolt dissipated harmlessly into the air. But obviously it was powerful, with an effective range of two thousand feet — twice that of the Anglese defense.

Toroh's plan now became apparent. He could batter the Anglese coast projectors while still beyond reach of them, and then make his landing. The cages over the barges were for protection from the smaller thunderbolts of the attacking aerial army.

George knew the cages were only partially effective. A bolt was difficult to aim, but it did queer things when it struck. From a short distance — a hundred feet or less — the barges could be set on fire and sunk. Their thin metal hulls were not protected. They could be pierced. The wooden super-structure could be fired; the swimming dogs struck and killed.

In hurried whispers Loto was constantly talking with Fahn back in the cavern. The Scientist's orders he repeated with his electrically magnified voice that could be heard easily by every one of the little aerial army.

For a time they circled about, above the barges, but keeping well beyond the two-thousand foot range. Against the blue of the sky their figures must have shown plainly to the Noths. Occasionally a bolt would flash up — harmless at that distance. And the barges pushed steadily forward.

At last Fahn decided the moment for attack had arrived. Loto repeated the order. George's division and Mogruud's separated from the rest. One hundred turned seaward, the others toward the land.

They dropped swiftly — straight down, like divers heavily laden with lead, dropping through water. And then — a darting, twisting swarm of insects — from every side at once they attacked the leading barge.

In the depths of the cavern at Anglese City, Fahn sat in his room of mirrors. A metal band about his head held a receiver to his ear. A black mouthpiece hung against his chest; by lowering his head he could bring his lips to it. Rogers was at his side. The mirrors in every part of the room were lighted — the viewpoints of the coast towers near the mouth of the channel. In several of the mirrored scenes, over the distant water and in the air, black specks were visible — the enemy and Fahn's army above it.

But these were not the vital crystal mirrors. A small one — a foot square perhaps — stood on the table before Fahn. He and Rogers were gazing into it intently. The mirror was connected with a tiny lens strapped to Loto's forehead; it gave Loto's viewpoint of the battle — showed the scene exactly as Loto saw it.

Fahn was silent — a stern, anxious old man, with

all his science around him, sitting in seclusion to direct this warfare upon which the fate of his people depended. Occasionally he would murmur something to Rogers; and the other man would speak into a mouthpiece — an order for the operator of the broadcasted aerial voices, controlled from another part of the cavern. Then throughout the island, cheering words to the Bas would resound — news of the progress of the battle. But Fahn's gaze at the little mirror never wavered.

George's and Mogruud's divisions descended upon the leading barge. The barge spat forth its bolts, but it could discharge only one or two against a hundred of the tiny ones of its attackers. Looking down, from Loto's viewpoint overhead, the barge was assailed on every side by the pencils of electrical flame. Figures dropped inert into the water; others, wounded, wavered upward. The wire cage over the barge was sizzling and crackling; the swimming dogs, a dozen or more of them, crumpled in the water and were dragged forward in their harness by the others.

The engagement had lasted no more than a minute when the air about the barge was suddenly plunged into blackness. Everything down there was blotted out — a patch of solid ink on the sea. The Noth vessel had exploded a bomb whose etheric vibration absorbed all light over a radius of five hundred feet from its source.

Fahn smiled grimly. The darkness there would pass presently. His own leaders, Loto, George, Mogruud and the two girls, were so equipped. Each of them could discharge such a bomb — a puff of darkness, cloaking everything around them in temporary invisibility.

Fahn heard his own orders roared by Loto. The attacking figures came up. But there were not two hundred of them now — a score perhaps lay down there in the water. A dozen more were wounded; a few were moving slowly homeward through the air.

Around the attacked Noth vessel the darkness still hung. But it was thinning out; in it now the vague outlines of the barge could be seen. Within a minute the dark patch was gone. One end of the barge was blazing; but the Noths were extinguishing the flames. Other figures were cutting loose the dead dogs in the water — dogs were leaping overboard to take their places.

The attacked barge presently moved onward; slowly, inexorably, they were all coming down the coast. They were no more than a mile or two now from the estuary of the channel-mouth.

Three times more Fahn ordered a division down at the same barge. The Noth tactics were repeated. The barge discharged a few of its bolts and then enveloped itself in blackness — an absence of light that even the thunderbolts could not illumine.

These brief engagements were largely a matter of individual action. Warfare was new to the Anglese, but they were learning. The huge bolts from the barge could not parallel for long the water level; inevitably they turned downward to discharge themselves. Close to the water the attackers were comparatively safe.

When the Anglese came up after these attacks and re-formed themselves in orderly array, there were but ten more of their number missing. But it was fifty in all; and a score of wounded.

The attacked barge now was blazing end to end. Its crowded deck was a turmoil of figures. They were plunging overboard — men and dogs — to avoid the flames. In a moment the barge tilted upward at its stern. Its torn bow was admitting the water; it slid downward, hissing, and disappeared beneath the surface. Figures bobbed up from the swirl — inert, charred figures; and others among them, still alive, swam about in aimless confusion.

One barge! But there were five others. And these others had all pushed forward until now they were almost down to the channel. Fahn realized that there were five hundred Noths and as many dogs crowded upon each of them. They could take to the water when still beyond range of his coast projectors and come forward swimming individually — each man mounted upon his dog. The coast defense could strike down no more than a few of them if they came in that fashion. Twenty-five hundred men and giant brutes, landing on the island.

Azeela and Dee were hovering close to Loto; they were asking their father's permission to try a new plan. The battle could not be maintained as it was going; the hand thunderbolt globes held but ten charges each, and the equipment of each individual was only three globes. A third of the thunderbolts were already exhausted in sinking one barge.

Fahn's expression did not change; only the grip of his fingers as he clenched them and the rising muscles under his thin cheeks betokened his emotion. His voice was steady, grim, as always, when he ordered his daughters to their desperate venture.

Azeela and Dee, with their twenty-six comrades, selected the barge that was now leading. In a closely knit group they hovered above it. Its thunderbolt shot up, but could not reach them. From the girls a pure-white beam of light shot downward — twenty-six tiny rays blending into one. Rogers, bending over Fahn to gaze into the little mirror, was amazed. Unlike any beam of light he had ever seen, this one was curved. It descended from the girls in a slightly bent bow, ending at the barge.

Fahn whispered a swift explanation to Rogers. To the Noths, looking upward along the beam, it would not appear curved, but straight The figures of the girls, by an optical illusion, would be seen, not where they actually were, but to one side.

The girls held their curved white ray steady. And plunging down the beam, following its slightly curved path, were the figures of Azeela and Dee.

The Noths saw them coming; a dozen bolts leaped into the air, one upon the other; but they flashed harmlessly to one side of their mark.

Within twenty seconds the two girls were close to the barge; yellow-red spurts of flame leapt from their weapons — flame that could be hurled thirty feet but no farther. It enveloped the barge — licking, seething, burning liquid gases that withered everything they touched. A puff of darkness which the retreating girls had left behind them blotted out the scene; and out of it an instant later Azeela and Dee came safely. The shaft of light from the girls above was extinguished as the two mounted to join them.

When light came again around the barge, it was sinking. Soon the swirling water held nothing but black, twisted figures.

The maneuver could not be repeated successfully.

From the other barges the Noths would have seen the curved beam—understood it and made allowances for it. Azeela and Dee, triumphant and flushed with their success, pleaded to try it again; but Fahn would not let them.

The afternoon was waning; the western sky was red; overhead clouds were gathering. And then Fahn ordered a general attack on all the barges.

The sun had set; the twilight deepened into night —a night of flashing lights, crackling artificial thunder; spurts of lurid flame; hissing of fire against water. At intervals, rockets came up; bursting, they cast a blue-white glare that for the space of a minute illumined for the Noths the menacing, darting figures.

The atmospheric disturbance of the past hours suddenly brought from the sky an electrical storm. Nature, more powerful than man, shot forth her own bolts to add to the din. They were in character very different from the harnessed, man-made lightning. Forked, jagged, crackling with their nearness, they leaped downward out of the low-hanging clouds.

The storm was brief as it was severe. It swept away. The moon had risen blood-red; it cast now its lurid light over the water — a full moon, transmuted through gold to silver as it mounted higher.

Another Noth vessel had been sunk. There were but three of the barges afloat. They were in distress. Many of their swimming dogs lay dead in the harness. Aboard all three of them, figures were fighting with flames. They clustered in a group near the center of the channel.

Loto had withdrawn his forces, reduced now to half their original number. With ammunition almost exhausted, they hovered out of range above their adversaries. The wounded were still straggling back through the air; a few of them already had arrived at the cavern.

Again Fahn ordered his army down. It would be the last attempt.

In the cavern room of mirrors, Fahn had not moved from his seat for hours. Often he could not see the battle plainly, for Loto, disobeying orders, had many times cast himself into the thick of it.

But now Loto was aloft; by the moonlight and

the glare of the rockets and bombs, Fahn saw that another Noth vessel had appeared — a very small barge. It was close inshore, coming swiftly forward and from it little objects of gleaming silver were mounting. One after the other they came sailing up.

Fahn rasped an order; Loto's voice roared it out. The men and girls who were descending to the attack halted, circling about — wondering what had happened.

The first of the white objects came sailing horizontally across the channel. It was moving slowly. It seemed to be a whirling white disc some foot or two in diameter.

Loto was still some distance away from it when a group of girls passed between him and the disc. The thing seemed to turn toward them. One of the girls became confused; it struck her. She fell. The disc, its rotation halted, fell also. Loto saw then what it was — broad, thin, crossed blades of steel, inclined to each other like the blades of a propeller. It had mounted and sustained itself in the air by its rotation. Loto remembered the defeat of the flying thunderbolt platforms which Fahn had sent northward to Toroh's encampment. These whirling knives were what had destroyed them!

The newly arrived barge was now sending up in every direction a slow but steady stream of the whirling knives. They seemed so easy to avoid that the aerial army at first paid them little heed. Loto's warning from Fahn rang out; but it came almost too late. The knives sought out the figures in the air. They began falling—cut, mangled by the whirling blades. There was confusion. The army mounted; but other knives had been sent straight upward and were floating down. Uncannily, they seemed to single out their victims.

Fahn understood now. This was the weapon Toroh had procured from that time-world of the past. These whirling knives were strangely, powerfully magnetized; they followed the human bodies passing near them, seeking contact.

The Scientist leader had ordered his fighters to the sea level; the knives as they came lower seemed to have spent themselves. They could be avoided. But nearly forty of the Anglese had met death before the lesson was learned.

The three larger barges were again advancing toward the Anglese coast. Without warning, without orders from Fahn, the little remnant of girls led by Azeela and Dee, darted at them. It was a movement, not fool-hardy, but well and swiftly planned. The girls, holding close to the surface, got themselves between two of the barges. The Noths could not fire, for they would have struck each other. A puff of inky darkness spread; out of it at close range jets of fire sprang at the Noths; then the girls came back. One of the Noth vessels was a mass of flames; the other two wavered — began retreating.

For a moment there was silence and darkness, lighted only by the moon and the flickering light from the blazing barge. The whirling blades were no longer being launched; the Anglese were again poised in the air.

Fahn had ordered that the small barge be attacked when, abruptly, from it a low hum sounded. George and Loto were hovering together at the moment; the barge was some five hundred feet below them and slightly off to one side. There seemed no dogs on it; only a few men under its wire cage, and a single large piece of apparatus.

The hum grew louder, more intense, as though some gigantic dynamo had been set into motion.

"What's that?" George demanded.

But Loto did not know.

Mogruud, with the remains of his division, was in the air half a mile away. He was on the other side of the small barge; his men, moving in scattered groups, began passing over it.

The hum was rising in pitch, up the scale until it became a shrill electrical scream. Mogruud's men wavered — struggled as though to avoid being pulled downward.

Then Loto knew what it must be — the rest of the apparatus Toroh had secured out of the past — a giant electromagnet of some unknown variety. It was pulling at every figure in the air — drawing them irrresistibly toward it.

Loto and George could feel the pull — invisible fingers snatching at them. The girls near at hand were fighting against it. Mogruud was coming forward with an effort, like a swimmer struggling

322

with the clutch of an undertow. Several of his men, closer to the barge, had been drawn to it — flattened helplessly against its wire caging. Fire was leaping from their burning bodies. They were electrocuted.

In the cavern Fahn sat tense, impotent. He could hear, as plainly as though out there over the sea, the scream of that uncanny thing that was reaching out its invisible electrical fingers to gather in its victims.

At his side, for an hour past, Rogers had been operating the larger mirrors — flashing into them scenes from the various towers along the coast. Now Fahn heard him give a sharp, horrified exclamation.

Rogers was staring at a mirrored scene from a coast tower near Orleen. Moonlight; purple, starry sky; the deep purple of the channel; to one side, the dim outlines of the Orleen houses. And from the channel off Orleen, lights were flashing; a bomb burst; its glare showed crowded barges close inshore! One of them, already at the beach, was disgorging its men and brutes!

323

CHAPTER XXVIII.

A NIGHT OF CONFUSION.

ONCE again, Toroh's trickery was disclosed. To Fahn, the tactics of the Noths in the battle off Anglese City were now understandable. This Noth attack, at which Fahn had hurled all his armed forces, had been no more than a ruse to cover up Toroh's main offensive at Orleen.

Toroh's orders, doubtless, had been to prolong the engagement, until, under cover of night, his main forces could effect their landing at the other end of the island. This small barge with the magnet had perhaps been ordered to slip by — hugging the north shore of the channel — and proceed to Orleen. But its commander had, at what he must have considered a decisive moment, used it against the remnant of the little aerial army.

Toroh's landing at Orleen was taking place; the channel expedition had served its purpose. The two remaining barges off Anglese City were in full re-

324

treat toward the open sea. The smaller barge, with its screaming magnet, was heading swiftly down the channel toward Orleen. The figures in the air were struggling against its pull. Some were losing, being hurled forward with control of themselves lost; others were forcing their way down to the water-level where the attraction seemed less. Still others had succeeded in escaping upward beyond range. High overhead they circled, seeking some way of helping their unfortunate comrades.

The double disaster was more than Fahn could cope with, or even watch closely in the two mirrors. Orleen lay on a peninsula some ten miles broad — water on three sides of it. The Noths were landing, spreading around the shores; across the land from shore to shore they were massed, but as yet they had not entered the city. Thousands of Arans were there — the king and his royal family — penned like rats in a trap. And there was only the small cavern with its meagre garrison of Scientists to defend them.

George found himself near the outer edge of the magnetic attraction. He could see the figures in the air nearer the barge, struggling to escape from it. He did not know where Loto was; or Azeela or Dee. He saw Mogruud, with fifteen or twenty of the Bas about him. They were passing swiftly below.

George wondered what he should do. The two larger barges were withdrawing. Some of the aerial figures were following them. George started that way, uncertainly. The figures were attacking the barges, from low, near the surface of the water. Mogruud and his men were there now. George hastened.

This last attack of the Anglese was one of desperate fury. George could see the flash of the bolts, close to the water. One of the barges must have fired through its own darkness and struck its mate. As the blackness cleared, George saw that both the Noth vessels were blazing. One of them sank a moment later; from the flames on the other, figures were plunging into the water.

The Anglese — one of them mounting — cast loose a light-bomb. In the brilliant glare, the aerial figures were darting about over the surface of the water, seeking out the Noth men and dogs who were swimming toward the island—striking them with the little thunderbolts, or with spurts of yellow red flame at closer range. George arrived to join them. It was ghastly, but necessary work. He used his weapons until they were exhausted.

The battle was won—all but the giant magnet. In the distance its blood-curdling scream still sounded.

And then George saw Dee. She had been several thousand feet up, flying with another girl, when the magnet was first put into operation. They were not close enough to feel its pull. A whirling knife had approached them; it struck the other girl—killed her. It was spent, but a corner of it had knocked Dee's motor-cylinder from her hand. She had begun floating down. Ever since she had been trying to swim through the air, with arms and legs kicking, she had fought to sustain herself.

She was almost at the surface when George saw her struggling ineffectually like a swimmer exhausted. He darted to her and gathered her into his arms. His cylinder drew them both upward.

"Dee," he whispered. "My little Dee! You're safe!"

Loto had dropped close to the surface. The magnet was pulling him; but with his cylinder held against it, he could make headway. The magnet now had done most of its work; those in the air had either succumbed, or escaped beyond range.

To one side, Loto could see the attack on the other two barges. Fahn's voice in his ear told him of the landing at Orleen. The Scientist ordered them all back. They were needed at Orleen; they must return.

But the magnet barge was heading down the channel. It would be used at Orleen. It must be stopped—destroyed now. Loto disobeyed Fahn. He headed for the little barge.

It was a plunge of no more than a few minutes. Soon Loto was well within the magnetism; he could not withdraw now. He tried to think clearly. Those others of the Anglese who had met this death, had lost control of themselves in the air. They had plunged forward, struggling, whirling so that they had not been able to use their weapons.

Loto had no thunderbolts remaining. His only weapon was the flaming liquid gas which he could project some fifty feet.

Just above the surface, head first, like an arrow he slid forward through the air. He did not fight against the magnet; he used his cylinder only to keep himself from turning sidewise.

He was conscious of the dark outlines of the barge rushing at him. He fired his jet of flame; but though he did not know it then, he had fired too soon. The flames fell short. A downward thrust of his cylinder power forced him upward. He barely missed the wire caging as his body shot over it — past it.

The magnet's scream was deafening. The Noths on the barge had fired a small thunderbolt between the wires, but had missed the swiftly passing mark.

Loto's momentum carried him a hundred feet or more beyond the barge. The magnet stopped him, drew him swiftly back. He was turning over now. He had lost control of himself. The sea, the sky, the approaching barge — were mingled in whirling confusion. He knew he could never escape; he must

329

strike the magnet with his flame, this time or never. A moment more and his body would be electrocuted against the cage.

A tiny bolt cracked past him. He turned over again, righted himself momentarily, and fired. The electrical scream died into abrupt silence; the flames had caught the magnet, burned out its coils.

Released suddenly, Loto's body shot upward with the pull of his cylinder. The cage, with flames spreading under it, dropped away beneath him.

He righted himself, and at a distance of about three hundred feet, hung poised. The flames spread over the barge; its few Noth figures plunged frantically into the water.

Loto mounted upward to join his comrades. Barely seventy-five of the original three hundred and twenty-eight, were left. Ten of them were girls. Loto found Azeela safe. George still carried Dee in his arms.

The flames from the burning barges died out; the silent moonlit channel was strewn with floating bodies. It seemed almost futile to search for their wounded; but they descended, and for a time moved about near the surface. Two they found still alive —one burned, the other, a girl, mangled by a flying knife.

Silently, with their burdens, they took their way back through the air to the cavern.

It was a night of confusion. The Noths were clustered around Orleen, waiting for the dawn before they entered the city. They were still coming across the channel—swimming dogs, mounted by men. All night they came. The puny garrison of the Orleen Cavern was powerless to stop them. It exhausted its bolts; it began sending out calls for help.

The Bas around Anglese City were mobilizing with their dogs. Hastily Fahn equipped them with weapons—hand thunderbolts and flame projectors. An hour and a half before dawn they were ready to start—an almost hopeless attempt to stem the horde of invaders who now held the entire west end of the island.

The little rag-end of aerial army that returned from the battle was exhausted, but in a few hours, it too, was ready to start.

Fahn, with his two daughters, and Rogers, Loto

and George, took the Frazia plane. On its platform Fahn mounted a single projector — the most powerful he possessed.

They started an hour before dawn — silent as they gazed down at the island of palms that was passing beneath them. They overtook their Bas army — left it behind them. In the air, back over Anglese City, tiny specks showed that the aerial army was starting. Above the hum of the Frazia motors, aerial voices of the Anglese City radio sounded — voices that told the Bas peasants living between the two cities to come eastward. They were obeying; little groups of refugees — old men, women and children — were moving backward along all the roads. Ahead in the sky occasional flashes shot up from Orleen.

"The Arans went there to avoid the deluge," Rogers said suddenly; and his laugh was grim.

But no one answered him.

Behind them presently the eastern sky was brightening. Loto was driving the plane, with Rogers beside him. The daylight grew — began reddening.

"Father! See, there is Orleen!"

CHAPTER XXIX.

THE DAY OF THE DELUGE.

THE second largest city of the island, Orleen, lay in a hollow, with twin peaks close behind it, the mouth of the channel and the gulf in front and to the sides. It was an Aran city, more beautiful even than the capital.

The plane, flying high, was circling. Loto's gaze went to the dawn. An omen of bloodshed! Azeela had called the crimson moon that, the night of the Festival. It was more than an omen — this dawn. The sun came up a huge, distorted ball of crimson fire, with lines of flame radiating from it to the zenith. A dark mass of rain cloud, hanging low above Orleen, lost its blackness as it soaked up the crimson light. The sky, even to the western horizon, was steeped in blood; the water reflected it; the air itself seemed to hold it suspended.

"The day of the deluge," murmured Loto. "The blood that will be spilled to-day —"

As though to symbolize his words, the cloud above Orleen began spilling its rain. And as the water fell, it caught the crimson sunlight—a myriad tiny drops of blood falling upon the Aran city.

The storm was transitory; the rain cloud swept past; but the blood in the sky remained.

In the hour that had passed since the plane left Anglese City, the Noths had occupied Orleen. Its cavern was taken. The Noth men and dogs stood in solid ranks around the mountain base; the beaches were black with them. Across the channel they were still coming—riders mounted upon swimming dogs—an occasional barge.

There were no sounds of thunderbolts in the city —no flashes. But as the plane descended, human sounds were heard—faint screams. And the city streets were in confusion.

Fahn was staring down into the city through spectacles with lenses mounted in short black tubes. He murmured something that his companions did not catch. His face was white and set; he was struggling to hold his composure.

"Descend, Loto. They are not armed with thunderbolts; those are all with Toroh and his men in the cavern."

The plane glided down, circling low above the city. The scene of carnage there became a series of brief, fragmentary pictures. Above the drone of the Frazia motors, the snarling of fighting dogs sounded; the screams of men and women, the shrill treble of children — human screams of death agony from the fangs of brutes tearing at them.

The plane passed low above a city street, following its length to the blue water that lapped on the white sand at its end. The street seemed full of dogs. A Noth rider — sinister, animal-like with his black bound head and his naked torso covered with black hair — arrived at a silent white house, with its white columns, splashing fountain, and vivid trellised flowers. The Noth dismounted, rushed into the house; he came out dragging an Aran woman — flung her white body to the eager, snarling brute. At the beach hundreds of terrified Arans sprang into the water; but the dogs followed them, pulled them under, released them at last, and the surf flung back their mangled bodies to the sand.

There was a public square, where a hundred or more Arans had gathered. The dogs charged them —tore at them—flung them into the air—fought over their broken bodies long after life had gone.

To every corner of the city the dogs spread simultaneously. A child climbed a pergola—a little Aran boy, white skinned, with long golden curls and a plump baby face. The dogs could not reach him. A Noth man climbed up, pulled him down.

Loto had given the Frazia controls to his father. With a small thunderbolt globe at his belt he went to the platform outside the cabin. Presently he found Azeela beside him. Her arm was around him; together they clung to their insecure footing, watching the scenes below as the plane made its swift circle over the city.

What could Fahn do? The thunderbolt projector, here on the platform, could kill a few Noths —a few dogs here and there. But of what avail among these hordes? The Orleen Cavern? Could they attack that? Toroh was probably there in the cavern. If they could kill him, these Noth barbarians, without a leader—

Confused and sick from what he was seeing, Loto tried to force Azeela into the cabin, but the white lipped girl would not go. The plane approached a house where on the roof top an Aran woman crouched with two little girls huddled at her feet. A Noth appeared from below, dashed at them across the roof. Beneath the eaves a dozen dogs stood with bared, dripping fangs held upward.

The plane was almost over the house. Loto pointed his globe downward, pressed its lever. There was a flash; a miniature crack of thunder; the globe recoiled in his hand. On the roof top the Noth man and the Aran woman and her children lay dead. The woman's white robe was blackened; the children's bodies were black — shriveled; a cornice of the building was ripped off; the woodwork was blazing.

It was so useless! Loto flung the globe from him, loathing it for having killed that woman and her little girls. He drew Azeela back with him into the cabin.

The king's palace of Orleen stood near the water front, in the midst of broad, magnificent gardens.

A mob of Noths surged around it, into the lower doors, on the balconies and roof top. As the plane passed overhead, its occupants caught a fleeting glimpse of the queen and her children, the girl wives of the king and the king himself — in the face of death with petty barriers at last broken down — all huddled together in a corner of the roof. The Noths rushed at them — broad, heavy swords flashing.

The plane swept past.

The twin peaks of Orleen stood six hundred feet apart, just behind the city. The one that housed the cavern had a broad, circular base, with a ragged, volcanic looking cone above. The other peak was considerably higher; it looked down upon its fellow.

To the higher of the peaks Fahn had directed Rogers to fly the plane. The Scientist had hardly spoken. He was pale, grim as ever, but his gaze upon his daughters held a curious softness. What were his plans. What were they going to do? George asked the questions; but Fahn ignored them.

The little aerial army approaching from Anglese City was now in sight. Fahn's radio spoke to it. He ordered it back, and ordered it to descend and stop the Bas army and its dogs. All of them were to return to the capital.

The plane landed on a small level rock near the summit of the higher peak. Over the cavern, six hundred feet away, a solitary male figure stood. The blood light of the sunrise fell full upon it. Toroh! He was standing there, regarding the city.

Fahn leaped to the projector; but Toroh had disappeared.

"Hurry!" exclaimed the Scientist. He still would not let them question him. He was unlashing the projector; they helped him lower it to the ground. He leaped down after it, adjusting it, swinging it to bear down upon the lower peak.

"We must hurry," he repeated. He was back on the cabin platform. "They will be out of the cavern, firing upon us."

The Noths down there were gazing up; others were now pouring out of the cavern entrance.

Fahn's projector was trained on the crater of the lower mountain. From this greater height its depths were visible.

In the cabin of the plane the Scientist's arms went

around his daughters. "Good-by, my girls — for a little time," he whispered in their own tongue.

They were frightened; suddenly Dee was crying. But he pushed them from him. He would attack the cavern; they must all stay in the plane — rise high — very high.

Something in the man's look — the command in his voice — struck them all silent. They obeyed. He climbed down to the rock. The plane's helicopters drew it swiftly into the air.

The sun was above the eastern horizon; the sky seemed an inverted bowl of blood. Beneath the plane Fahn's figure, standing beside his projector, showed clear cut against the black rock under him. At the base of the cavern-mountain Noths had appeared with apparatus. They were adjusting it hurriedly.

A blue-white flash from Fahn's projector spat downward across the six hundred feet and into the crater mouth. Thunder rolled out. Another flash. Another — until they became almost continuous. Far down in the earth within the crater the slumbering forces there began to answer. A rumbling sounded — a low, ominous muttering, pregnant with infinite power. Steam hissed upward; a puff of smoke —

The plane had been ascending rapidly; it was thousands of feet up now. Fahn's thunderbolts persisted; and at last the angered fires of the earth were unleashed. The mountain seemed to split apart; the report was deafening; flaming gases, cinders and ashes were hurled upward and outward.

The main force of the explosion was sidewise toward the city; but even so the plane barely avoided the torrent of molten rock and blazing gas that mounted from below.

The city was engulfed in flame over which a heavy smoke hung like a pall. A tremendous lake of viscous liquid fire lay where the peaks and the cavern once had been. The earth was rumbling, shaking, splitting apart. The scene was vague — dull with a lurid red glare that struggled with the blackness of the smoke.

A moment, and a rift appeared. The smoke seemed to part, roll aside. Through the rift the burning city showed for an instant clear and distinct — the crowded city in which now no single human or beast could have remained alive.

Still not content, the earth was heaving over the whole western end of the island. And from the sea a great tidal wave came rolling up over the sinking land — hissing, quenching the fires, obscuring everything in a cloud of steam. Like a mist the steam presently dissipated. The turgid waters lashed themselves into furious waves that gradually were stilled.

It was daylight — sullen red day — with only the wreckage on the waters — charred fragments of bodies, thousands of them floating for miles around — mute evidence of what had gone before.

CHAPTER XXX.

THE RETURN.

ONCE again the plane hung like a shimmering ghost above the towering piles of steel and masonry — New York City at the peak of its civilization. To Azeela and Dee it had been a brief trip of awe and wonder — a trip northward through space and back through time.

After the cataclysm, they had stayed but a week back in Anglese City. The entire western end of the island had sunk into the gulf, carrying Toroh and his Noths and the Arans and their king to destruction. In Anglese City a new government was formed — a democracy of the Bas, with Mogruud at its head.

Rogers was impatient to return to his wife in the New York City of his birth. Azeela and Dee, left orphans, had no wish to stay. Unobtrusively as it had come, the Frazia plane departed.

In the humming, glowing cabin of the plane the

voyagers were waiting for the dials to reach the time world for which they were heading. On one of the side benches, the ghostlike figures of Loto and Azeela sat a little apart from the others; they were talking softly as they gazed down through the window beside them.

"You think Mogruud will make a good leader?" she asked. "My father would have been so strong — stern, but always just and fair —" Her eyes had filled with tears.

He pressed her hand sympathetically. "I know, Azeela. But you mustn't grieve. He gave his life for his people —"

"Yes. And he said 'Good-by — for a little time.' Oh, Loto — I did not realize then what he meant."

"He knew — beyond this life — you would be with him again. And you will." His arm went around her tenderly. "I shall always try to make you happy. I promise it, Azeela. Always, as long as we live."

"Beloved," she murmured. "Beloved, who always understands."

Rogers had been talking to George and Dee. He

left them to attend to the motors. Dee was watching the scene beneath the plane. As they fled back through the centuries the great city was melting away.

"Your city that we're going to," she said after a long silence, "George, is it like this? Are we almost to its time now?"

"No," he laughed. "It's a very little, puny city I have to show you, Dee. I used to think it was wonderful! But it's only a conceited child—learning as fast as it can and thinking it knows everything. I used to be like that myself. But this sort of trip changes one."

She did not answer.

"I'm glad you're coming back with us, Dee."

"Yes," she said abstractedly.

"Dee," he persisted out of another silence, "I wonder if you know how happy it makes me to have you—here where we're going? I've wanted to tell you for a long time. I mean—maybe you don't know how I feel. I—"

On this return journey the plane had now reached

the height of its time velocity. The swiftly changing form of the city blurred the scene into a confusion of shifting details, among which only the broadest fundamentals were discernible. The northern section of Central Park presently lay open. Then the great building that covered its southern end melted into nothingness; and trees and water were in its stead.

George was at the dials. "One hundred years! We're almost into our own century!"

Through decreasing intensities of the Proton current, they slackened their time velocity. The park, whitened with winter, turned green again as the previous summer was reached. Soon the days separated from the nights. The sun came up from the west, plunged swiftly across the sky, and dropped into the east.

It was spring, but the retrogression soon brought winter again. A January snowfall lay white beneath the naked trees of the park. But it was autumn in a moment.

Rogers was watching the dials closely. Summer again; then spring. In one of the brief periods of night he threw the switch to the first intensity. The plane began drifting to the south. The dim stars were swinging eastward, overhead in a murky sky. The city lights shone yellow.

The roof of the Scientific Club came into view among the buildings south of the plane. Rogers threw off the current completely.

"Look, Dee!" cried George. "Look, Azeela! There it is at last! See the board enclosure?"

CHAPTER XXXI.

THE NEW LIFE.

A n evening in March. In the large living room of the Banker's Park Avenue apartment, a group of his friends were gathered. Dinner was over; a dignified butler was serving coffee; the men were lighting their cigars.

A matured woman and four men — all in evening dress — were sitting in a group; mingled with their voices came the soft, limpid tones of a piano. It stood in a secluded alcove — a grand piano of carved mahogany. On a bench before its keyboard, a young man in a Tuxedo was sitting playing. George. Dee stood beside him, leaning against the instrument. She was gazing at the page of music with a puzzled frown; then at his fingers as they roamed the keys, and then, in admiration, at his face.

On a high-back davenport before an open fireplace, Loto sat with Azeela. There was an artificial black flower in her spun gold hair — the mourning custom of her time world. Her milk-white throat was bare; her clinging blue dress made her seem taller and older, and the blue was mirrored in her eyes. She was silent, staring into the flames licking upward from the huge logs.

"That's very pretty music," she said finally. "So big an instrument—this piano as you call it—you never would think one could play it."

"Chopin," he answered. "A piece by Chopin. George plays Chopin mighty well. Azeela, there is so much I have to show you. Just that one little thing—Chopin, for instance. I want you to hear the music of some of the great composers—and our pianists."

"And the opera," she prompted. "And you promised you would take me to a theater."

"I will, of course. There are so many things for you to see. Why, it will be just like a new world— a new life that you're just beginning, Azeela."

"Yes," she murmured. "A new life, in a new world. It seems like that already."

"And wait till you ride in the subways and tubes! You'll be surprised how—"

But she shuddered. "I do not believe I want to do that. It would bring back memory of the cavern — other things."

George and Dee left the piano and advanced to the fireplace. Azeela moved over on the davenport. Loto stood up; but George shook his head.

"Thanks. Dee and I thought we'd try the window seat."

Across the room the Big Business Man, the Doctor, and the Banker were demanding additional details from Rogers.

"That Toroh and his Noths were in the cavern at Orleen," the Banker said gruffly. "Can't you keep the thing straight? I want to hear it consecutively — not jump around in this way."

Ensconced in the window seat, George and Dee gazed out at the yellow lights of the city around them — a city so different from anything Dee could have even imagined.

There was a soft, shaded rose light beside the girl. George was not looking out of the window, but at her. He had seen Dee in many costumes, but never, he thought, was she so beautiful as right now.

A girl of his own time world. He had not realized that this was the way he had always wanted her to look. Her dress, dropping to a few inches above her silken ankles, was soft and clinging. There was a Roman sash about her waist. Her black hair, like Azeela's, was dressed on her head. Like Azeela, too, she wore the dark mourning flower. The soft light beside her threw a flush on her milk-white throat and cheeks.

Feeling his gaze, she turned.

"You like the way Lylda has clothed me? It feels very strange."

"Yes," he said. "You look — beautiful, Dee!"

She turned back to the window in confusion. From below, the hum of the city floated up to them; the raucous sirens of automobiles.

"Yes," he repeated. "I do like it very much, Dee. Your hair done up that way, especially."

Abruptly his arms were around her; he was kissing her.

"George! George! Some one will see you!"

"No," he protested. "No, they won't. Anyway, suppose they do? I don't care — do you?"

351

SCIENCE FICTION

An Arno Press Collection

FICTION

About, Edmond. **The Man with the Broken Ear.** 1872

Allen, Grant. **The British Barbarians:** A Hill-Top Novel. 1895

Arnold, Edwin L. **Lieut. Gullivar Jones:** His Vacation. 1905

Ash, Fenton. **A Trip to Mars.** 1909

Aubrey, Frank. **A Queen of Atlantis.** 1899

Bargone, Charles (Claude Farrere, pseud.). **Useless Hands.** [1926]

Beale, Charles Willing. **The Secret of the Earth.** 1899

Bell, Eric Temple (John Taine, pseud.). **Before the Dawn.** 1934

Benson, Robert Hugh. **Lord of the World.** 1908

Beresford, J. D. **The Hampdenshire Wonder.** 1911

Bradshaw, William R. **The Goddess of Atvatabar.** 1892

Capek, Karel. **Krakatit.** 1925

Chambers, Robert W. **The Gay Rebellion.** 1913

Colomb, P. et al. **The Great War of 189—.** 1893

Cook, William Wallace. **Adrift in the Unknown.** n.d.

Cummings, Ray. **The Man Who Mastered Time.** 1929

[DeMille, James]. **A Strange Manuscript Found in a Copper Cylinder.** 1888

Dixon, Thomas. **The Fall of a Nation:** A Sequel to the Birth of a Nation. 1916

England, George Allan. **The Golden Blight.** 1916

Fawcett, E. Douglas. **Hartmann the Anarchist.** 1893

Flammarion, Camille. **Omega:** The Last Days of the World. 1894

Grant, Robert et al. **The King's Men:** A Tale of To-Morrow. 1884

Grautoff, Ferdinand Heinrich (Parabellum, pseud.). **Banzai!** 1909

Graves, C. L. and E. V. Lucas. **The War of the Wenuses.** 1898

Greer, Tom. **A Modern Daedalus.** [1887]

Griffith, George. **A Honeymoon in Space.** 1901

Grousset, Paschal (A. Laurie, pseud.). **The Conquest of the Moon.** 1894

Haggard, H. Rider. **When the World Shook.** 1919

Hernaman-Johnson, F. **The Polyphemes.** 1906

Hyne, C. J. Cutcliffe. **Empire of the World.** [1910]

In The Future. [1875]

Jane, Fred T. **The Violet Flame.** 1899

Jefferies, Richard. **After London; Or, Wild England.** 1885

Le Queux, William. **The Great White Queen.** [1896]

London, Jack. **The Scarlet Plague.** 1915

Mitchell, John Ames. **Drowsy.** 1917

Morris, Ralph. **The Life and Astonishing Adventures of John Daniel.** 1751

Newcomb, Simon. **His Wisdom The Defender:** A Story. 1900

Paine, Albert Bigelow. **The Great White Way.** 1901

Pendray, Edward (Gawain Edwards, pseud.). **The Earth-Tube.** 1929

Reginald, R. and Douglas Menville. **Ancestral Voices:** An Anthology of Early Science Fiction. 1974

Russell, W. Clark. **The Frozen Pirate.** 2 vols. in 1. 1887

Shiel, M. P. **The Lord of the Sea.** 1901

Symmes, John Cleaves (Captain Adam Seaborn, pseud.). **Symzonia.** 1820

Train, Arthur and Robert W. Wood. **The Man Who Rocked the Earth.** 1915

Waterloo, Stanley. **The Story of Ab:** A Tale of the Time of the Cave Man. 1903

White, Stewart E. and Samuel H. Adams. **The Mystery.** 1907

Wicks, Mark. **To Mars Via the Moon.** 1911

Wright, Sydney Fowler. **Deluge: A Romance** *and* **Dawn.** 2 vols. in 1. 1928/1929

SCIENCE FICTION

NON-FICTION
Including Bibliographies,
Checklists and Literary Criticism

Aldiss, Brian and Harry Harrison. **SF Horizons.** 2 vols. in 1. 1964/1965

Amis, Kingsley. **New Maps of Hell.** 1960

Barnes, Myra. **Linguistics and Languages in Science Fiction-Fantasy.** 1974

Cockcroft, T. G. L. **Index to the Weird Fiction Magazines.** 2 vols. in 1 1962/1964

Cole, W. R. **A Checklist of Science-Fiction Anthologies.** 1964

Crawford, Joseph H. et al. **"333": A Bibliography of the Science-Fantasy Novel.** 1953

Day, Bradford M. **The Checklist of Fantastic Literature in Paperbound Books.** 1965

Day, Bradford M. **The Supplemental Checklist of Fantastic Literature.** 1963

Gove, Philip Babcock. **The Imaginary Voyage in Prose Fiction.** 1941

Green, Roger Lancelyn. **Into Other Worlds:** Space-Flight in Fiction, From Lucian to Lewis. 1958

Menville, Douglas. **A Historical and Critical Survey of the Science Fiction Film.** 1974

Reginald, R. **Contemporary Science Fiction Authors,** First Edition. 1970

Samuelson, David. **Visions of Tomorow:** Six Journeys from Outer to Inner Space. 1974